SHARDS
OF
MURDER

Also by Cheryl Hollon

Pane and Suffering

SHARDS
OF
MURDER

CHERYL
HOLLON

KENSINGTON PUBLISHING CORP.
http://www.kensingtonbooks.com

KENSINGTON BOOKS are published by

Kensington Publishing Corp.
119 West 40th Street
New York, NY 10018

Copyright © 2016 by Cheryl Hollon

All Kensington Titles, Imprints, and Distributed Lines are available at special quantity discounts for bulk purchases for sales promotions, premiums, fund-raising, and educational or institutional use. Special book excerpts or customized printings can also be created to fit specific needs. For details, write or phone the office of the Kensington special sales manager: Kensington Publishing Corp., 119 West 40th Street, New York, NY 10018, attn: Special Sales Department, Phone: 1-800-221-2647.

Kensington and the K logo Reg. U.S. Pat & TM Off.

ISBN-13: 978-1-61773-762-6
ISBN-10: 1-61773-762-3
First Kensington Mass Market Edition: March 2016

eISBN-13: 978-1-61773-763-3
eISBN-10: 1-61773-763-1
First Kensington Electronic Edition: March 2016

10 9 8 7 6 5 4 3 2 1

Printed in the United States of America

To my loving parents,
Wendell and Marcella Hollon

Acknowledgments

I'm such a lucky writer. The fates have granted me a team that works hard to bring the Webb's Glass Shop Mystery series to life. My agent, Beth Campbell of BookEnds, LLC, is my champion in all things practical in the crazy ever-changing world of publishing. My editor at Kensington, Mercedes Fernandez, has an infectious enthusiasm that inspires me to work harder to bring each book to a better place. I am so grateful for the creativity that marketing manager Morgan Elwell brings to the team in spreading the word through advertising.

My freelance publicist at Breakthrough Promotions, PJ Nunn, and her marvelous team have lined up events and promotional venues that I love and truly appreciate.

I owe many thanks for the continuing support and inspiration of the Sisters in Crime online chapter, the Guppies (the Great Unpublished). The mystery-writing community is incredibly generous with time, energy, and advice.

Having a face-to-face critique group is an incredible resource for good guidance. We have been meeting since 2007 and continue to strengthen each other's work. Big thanks go to Amy Jordan, Krista Rickard, and Sam Falco. See you next month under the cone of silence.

Webb's Glass Shop is roughly based on the actual Grand Central Stained Glass shop owned by Bradley and Eloyne Erickson. Thank you both for many wonderful hours of instruction, advice, and patience. I am thankful to everyone who helped me make this story as accurate as possible, but any errors that remain are mine alone.

Without a doubt, I have been inspired to write by my personal muse, Joye Barnes. Her unfailing enthusiasm has spurred me to try harder and harder to tell a good story. When I'm stuck, I just imagine what Joye would like to hear and my fingers fly across the keys. Thanks as well to her close group of supportive friends at the woodland cottage.

Having the total support of my family is as important to me as the writing itself. I appreciate it Eric, Jennifer, Aaron, Beth, Ethan, Lena Rose, Mister, Pepper, Ricky, and Snowy.

My husband, George, is my biggest fan, a tireless supporter, my first reader, and the love of my life. He makes my heart sing.

Chapter 1

"You're going to love the Beach Blonde." Savannah raised her glistening pint of straw-colored beer to clink her former mentor Keith Irving's glass. "It reminds me of my favorite ale back in Seattle."

"You had a favorite? I seem to recall that you were determined to try a different beer every time we walked into a brewery."

Is he saying that I was flighty? When she had been Keith's student back in Seattle, she *had* been a little prone to fancy. She was always exploring new glass-working techniques before she had completely mastered the old ones. That must have been frustrating for him—he drew on an unlimited reserve of patience with her erratic experimentation.

Keith sipped the ale and his dark bushy eyebrows raised over his iris blue eyes. Putting his pint back on the beer mat, he looked around the 3 Daughters Brewing tasting room. "You have a point, though. This is as good as anything back home."

"Damn straight," Savannah grinned wide. It was a warm reminder of how much she desired his approval. She and Keith were sitting at a high top near the back of the tasting room. The noisy after-work happy hour crowd had gone and the Friday night date crowd hadn't yet arrived. That meant that the modern industrial décor felt cozy and intimate rather than raucous and cele-bratory.

Keith looked down into his beer. "My condo-lences on the death of your father. He was a significant loss to the stained glass world. I'm very sorry."

"Thank you, I appreciate that. I didn't realize how well respected he was until after he was gone."

"How are you coping?"

"Not as well as I would like. It was a—" She was startled by the tightening of her throat. It had already been a couple of months. "It was a diffi-cult time. It still is, for that matter. But now, I've got some great help. My office manager, Amanda Blake, is an outrageously cheerful person and I've taken on Dad's apprentice, Jacob Under-wood. He's incredibly talented, and the deep concentration required for the craft helps him manage life with Asperger's syndrome. Jacob is flourishing to the real benefit of Webb's."

"Is it true what I heard?" He tilted his head

slightly with a gentle smile. "That you were involved in the investigation of your father's death?"

Savannah wiped a hand across her forehead, then cupped her pint. "Yes, it turned out that both Dad and his longtime assistant were murdered. I arrived here planning to sell up and return to Seattle, but I was driven to decode the messages my father left behind. Dad had been a cryptographer for the government. The result of the adventure was that it helped the police catch the murderer. Everyone helped and I felt like I found my forever home."

"So, you not only dealt with the death of your father, but helped catch his murderer—I just can't imagine the emotional toll."

Savannah looked around the brewing house, taking a long moment to clarify her feelings. "It was a horrible experience, but oddly satisfying in the end. I learned some valuable lessons. First, I have some incredible friends who care about me. Second, the local business community has supported Webb's from the time my grandfather had a motorcycle business here in the twenties until my dad started the glass shop. My family inspired that."

Keith nodded slowly and sat silent for a few moments. "Speaking of Webb's, what's it like to go from student to business owner in a heartbeat?"

Savannah looked up at the ceiling, "Wow, you are literally correct with that one. I'm still struggling with the abrupt change of focus.

There are so many things that Dad took care of that I'm discovering surprise by surprise."

"It requires a totally different skill set from a carefree creative artist. The transition from student to master requires tremendous personal growth. Some can't do it. You appear to be doing fine."

Squirming in her seat, Savannah replied, "Carefree artist is a good description of my former self. I'm having difficulty with the role of community leader within the Grand Central District of St. Petersburg, Florida. I don't have a background in politics and it's all about relationships and history and things that I don't know about."

Keith leaned over, a conspiratorial glint in his eyes. "I'll tell you a secret. No one understands small-town politics."

Savannah laughed. "I'm so glad you're here. I've been tossed a huge speed bump. My dad's friends appointed me as the judge in the glass category for the Spinnaker Art Festival this weekend."

Keith was in town for the festival to support one of his current protégés in entering the competition. He already knew all about Savannah's appointment as a judge—and her nerves surrounding the job.

Keith chuckled. "As my former star pupil, I expect it won't take very much advice to bring you up to speed."

"Judging was not a part of your curriculum back

at the studio." She sipped her beer. "Seriously, how do I choose?"

"I've never found it difficult to choose a winner. My challenge has always been to keep from alienating the chief judge and the other artists. Innovation in the glass arts is not always of interest to the mainstream art collectors or appreciated by the organizational committee. Did they give you some guidelines to follow?"

"They didn't have time to give me anything. The original judge was going to be my dad. He was famous for his widely popular choices— he wouldn't have needed them. Their first replacement had a family emergency, so they turned on the charm and I accepted. I'm simply a last-minute solution."

"Do you think the reason they called on you as a judge was solely due to your dad's reputation?"

"Frankly, I think it was the safe thing to do. They could give it to me as a tribute to my dad's memory and give the snub to Frank Lattimer once again."

She named the owner of Webb's rival glass shop. Frank was not well loved in town, and his failed attempt to buy out Webb's during a vulnerable time was well known. Even though she was nervous about judging a competition, she was privately pleased that the festival committee had given their support to her over Frank.

Keith looked surprised. "Oh, come on now, you can't believe that. Surely they wouldn't go that far to insult him. He has a business right downtown with a huge display gallery."

"I don't know who in particular he has annoyed on the committee, but Frank can annoy even the most amiable of supporters." She paused, then admitted, "Honestly, in all practicality, they should have given him the job this year. I don't have very many qualifications other than being John Webb's poor orphan daughter."

"Don't sell yourself short. I can give you enough practical guidance to get you through the Spinnaker Art Festival—I've been judging for more years than I care to admit. But, in reality, all I can do is tell you how I approach judging." He grinned. "Judge for yourself what makes sense to you. Your instincts are good."

"If you say so." Savannah sipped her beer.

"I say so. Remember what I used to say?"

"Oh no, not a test! You were a fountain of inspirational quotes."

Keith chuckled. "Okay, but this one is true. 'Life begins at the end of your comfort zone.'" He paused and poked a finger into her upper arm. "You know that."

Savannah leaned away and nodded. "I remember that one. I've been living it."

"Anyway, first I walk around and get a quick look at each exhibit booth and see if any of them hit me emotionally without analyzing or thinking about it. That gives me a chance to see if there are any works that immediately stand out from the rest, and it has been my experience that the winner is usually among them. Later,

I stop in front of each booth and analyze what I see in design, color, and mastery of technique."

"That's easy enough."

"Also, if the technique is traditional, such as a Tiffany-style stained glass lamp, it should be a new approach. I always look for something unique showing me a deep understanding of the underlying principles, or a completely different twist on the ordinary."

"That sounds pretty straightforward."

"It should be—and that's the secret. A truly unique approach to glass should stand out like a flame in the darkness."

"Ugh, I'm terrified that I won't live up to Dad's reputation."

"Understandable, but no one would have more faith in your judgment." He covered her hand with his and gave it a light squeeze before letting go. "He was a great judge, but you're his daughter, and I have to tell you, the apple didn't fall far from the tree." He grinned widely, and Savannah smiled as well.

Maybe I have a natural instinct. That would be awesome.

"The timing couldn't be much worse." She ran a hand through her closely cropped curly black hair. "I'm starting a new weeklong workshop on Monday."

"Timing will never be right. What type of class?"

"This one teaches the major aspects of fused glass. I've got a monstrous new kiln installed along with one that Dad already had and we're almost ready to go. I haven't even tested the big one yet, but I'll do that this weekend. It has an electronic control panel to automate the timing and temperature changes for the firings. That makes the process less math intensive. Even better, we can let it run overnight and increase our production.

"That's good for both students and clients. The ones we use for teaching in the studio require hand calculations for glass size and a timer for changing the manual temperature settings. It's tedious, but the real purpose is to teach a thorough understanding of the principles of fusing."

"That's exactly the right approach." He touched her arm softly. "How about dinner?"

"Sorry, I'd like that but I'm totally distracted by everything that's swirling around right now. How about after the festival is over? I'll be in a much better mood."

She sensed a movement behind her.

"So, this is your mentor?" Edward pulled up a bar stool between Savannah and Keith. His posh British accent oozed smoothly from a thin frame in a black shirt over tight jeans tucked into tan rattlesnake Western boots. He extended a hand. "Hi, I'm Edward Morris, owner of the Queen's Head Pub, right next door to Webb's Glass Shop. I hear that you're the best hot glass teacher in the world."

Savannah widened her eyes. Edward must have stopped by to arrange for more beer for his pub. She didn't specifically invite him to meet

Keith here. Edward was not yet a lover—but definitely a strong candidate. Savannah's reticence was mostly because her feelings were still a mess of unresolved ex-boyfriend angst. Plus there was the complication that Edward had been a principal suspect in the murder of her father.

Keith stood and shook hands with the very tall man. "Keith Irving. I've heard about you, too."

They stood looking eye to eye. Savannah felt the tension sizzle while also realizing in a flash that both men were the same height.

Savannah patted Edward's stool. He took the hint and sat.

Keith sat and looked sideways at Edward. "Glad to hear the nice part of my reputation precedes me."

"There's a not nice part?"

Savannah smothered a huge cough with her hand, then rearranged her face to disguise the surprise and slight annoyance at Edward's comment. "Keith has the well-deserved reputation for destroying glasswork that doesn't meet his exacting artistic standards. I've left the studio shattered in every sense of the word more than once."

Keith stiffened his back a bit taller. "In truth, there's no room for the merely ordinary at Pilchuck Glass School. It's not helpful for the growth of a student to condone mediocrity. Remarkably, the threat of immediate destruction brings out their best work. For the naturally gifted"—he eyed Savannah—"it gives them amazing confidence to start a successful career as a true artisan."

Savannah grimaced over at Edward. "A lecture I've heard more than once."

Keith sipped his beer and looked at Edward over the rim. "I've heard about your escapades with Savannah as well. Helping her find the man who murdered her father is a task most would not have accepted."

"It was a team effort. We're a very close community here in the Grand Central District. Besides, an actual third-generation St. Petersburg native is as rare as bluebells in July. She deserves to be safe from harm."

Edward waved a hand to the bartender. "Hi, Mike, my regular pint of Brown Pelican, please." He turned to Keith. "So, other than the lovely Savannah, what brings you to town?"

Savannah looked sharply at Edward. *What's wrong with you?*

"Good question," said Keith. "I am a long way from home."

Savannah smiled and propped her chin into both hands.

Keith raised both hands in surrender. "I confess I'm here for more than just a visit to see a former student. Two of our students from Pilchuck have taken jobs with the local Chihuly Museum as interns to learn the business end of art."

"But I thought there was a program for that in Seattle," said Savannah.

"There is, but there aren't enough positions

for each student to have an opportunity to rotate through the program. It's not just learning about the various methods and history of the glassworks; they also learn to care for the exhibits and discover the harsh realities of an invisible monster named 'cash flow.' "

Edward squinted. "What do you mean by caring for the exhibits? They're all glass. They don't need to be fed or watered or anything."

Savannah and Keith looked at each other for a second. Keith motioned for Savannah to answer.

"It's extremely important that the glassworks in the museum stay dust free. It's not such an issue in Seattle, but here in hot, sandy Florida, it's quite a challenge. Each visitor brings in a bit of the outside and it's impossible to control that. So someone needs to dust the priceless and very fragile exhibits without breaking them. That's what students learn to do."

"Oh." Edward looked sheepish. "Duh."

"Don't feel bad." Savannah squeezed Edward's arm. "It's not particularly obvious."

"Anyway," said Keith, "I'm here to check up on the program and also to help one of them with setting up an exhibit booth tomorrow at Spinnaker."

"You have a student in the show?"

"Yes, he was admitted in good time so that we could arrange the intern position with the Chihuly Museum. Another of my former students, Megan Loyola, has also been accepted into the festival. She reminds me very much of you." Keith nodded toward Savannah.

"How so?"

"She's wicked smart and has a genius for inventing glass techniques to form something completely different and spectacular. I can't wait for you to see her work."

"Hey, you're not trying to influence a judge are you?"

Keith shook his head. "No chance. You are your father's daughter; he was unbelievably ethical. The interns are Vincent O'Neil and Leon Price. Vincent is a good craftsman with broad technical and mechanical knowledge. Leon, however, is a bit of an uptight urbanite and that rigidly controlled approach comes out in his work. They're sharing living and travel expenses. Leon is the one who has an exhibit booth at the Spinnaker Art Festival. Vincent applied, but didn't make the cut."

Edward shifted a bit and signaled the bartender for another round. He turned to Savannah. "Have you told Keith about your new project?"

"Not yet." She looked crossly at Edward. "I'm still in the investigation stage."

"What new project?" Keith drained the last of his beer.

"I'm going to open a new glass studio in this area. It will be the largest in the South once I've got it up and running."

"Wow, that's the kind of success we hope our

students will achieve after they leave. Will it be in this area of town?"

"Only a few blocks south of here in an up-and-coming new industrial park district. It will be an artist's loft space with reasonable rental rates on a month-by-month plan. As an incentive to the eternally cash-strapped prospective client, I'm offering the space without a long-term lease."

"How much square footage?"

"I'm thinking over ten thousand square feet. Part of that will be an exhibit space. That will give my students a transition phase between student and professional artist. There will also be a media room for presentations and tutorials."

Edward shifted in his seat. "But you're keeping the original Webb's as well?"

"Absolutely." She sipped her beer. "That building has been in the family forever and is the anchor store in that block. It's absolutely perfect for beginners—but not for the intermediate- to advanced-level artists."

"Wow, Savannah," said Keith with emotion cracking his voice. "I predicted great things from your skill and talent, but this fantastic news is beyond my expectations. What are you going to call it? Where is it going to be?"

"Webb's Studio is the working title I'm using until I register it as a business name and have my accountant file the corporation paperwork. He'll organize a name search to make sure it's unique, but I think it is." She smiled. "I've been looking at some available warehouse properties a little south of where we're sitting. I think I've found a candidate location."

Edward lifted his glass. "A toast to the success of Webb's Studio." The three glasses clinked in perfect harmony.

Chapter 2

Saturday Morning

The glass art entries in the Spinnaker Art Festival defined excellence. Savannah followed Keith's advice by walking through the entire breadth of the festival grounds from one end to the other. It was a warmish spring day, with barely enough cloud cover to keep the sun from baking the ground while she trawled the aisles. Her big, floppy straw hat kept her head cool when the sun peeked out in fits and starts. It matched her comfortable jute sandals that set off her only summer dress to perfection. Dressed up for judging in a floral cotton print, she felt very much like it was the first day of school—a little exposed, but excited to see what the day would bring.

The Spinnaker Art Festival juried show was the highlight of the winter season competitions on the art show circuit, and the selection committee admitted only a small percentage of the applicants.

This vibrant event featured over 200 artists chosen from more than 2,000 applicants. As a result, the caliber of the art was original, evocative, curious, and beautiful.

As the festival's popularity had increased in recent years, the festival site had moved to a larger waterfront park, Vinoy Park, located north of the traditional Straub Park on the downtown main drag of Beach Drive. The new location accommodated approximately fifty additional exhibit booths, and there was plenty of room for a large food court populated with local restaurants. The wine and beer offerings acted as an effective fundraiser for the festival and were doing a brisk business.

The festival map helpfully listed each glass artist with a location symbol next to the artist's name. As she walked by each booth, Savannah ticked off the name on the list. Every known discipline of glass was represented by at least one booth. The most popular type was stained glass, which ranged from lusciously designed Tiffany windows to sparsely elegant pieces in the Frank Lloyd Wright style. These were closely followed in popularity by fused glass pieces of gigantic puzzle piece platters down to complete service sets for sushi. There was even an entry featuring life-sized bird sculptures based on the drawings from the original Audubon watercolors. The artist had cleverly used prints of the paintings as a backdrop for each glass creation.

When she reached the last booth, Savannah

checked the list of names and discovered that she had missed two exhibits.

How did that happen?

Studying the map, she saw that she had overlooked a short aisle just left of the festival entrance. She crossed the park to add them to her initial survey. The small sector was definitely a bit out of the way and a tree blocked the line of sight to the rest of the festival.

That's going to annoy the artists. If I missed them, many paying customers will as well.

Traveling down the aisle, she looked for the missing artists' booths and finally reached the end to discover two glass artists directly across from each other. Their work was the most exciting that she had seen so far. One was a display of life-sized hollow body forms hanging from oversized industrial j-hooks and chains; the other exhibitor displayed huge glass vessels that had been hand blown and then etched in a Romanesque fashion. She stood and stared at one booth, then turned and stared at the other.

These two booths displayed skill and creativity yards above the rest. They belonged to Megan Loyola and Leon Price, the ex-student and one of the interns from Keith's studio in Seattle.

You were right, Keith, you know it when you see it. But you didn't mention that I might see more than one winner.

Determined to live up to her dad's reputation for fairness and his finely tuned eye for talent, Savannah walked by each glass exhibit booth and meticulously filled out the judge's evaluation form for each entrant. She didn't chat with the exhibitors, but tried smiling as often as she could to ease their fears. She remembered how terrified she felt while being judged for the first time—she had shaken so badly she momentarily feared she'd make the ground tremor.

The evaluation form was a new element in the judging process. It was supposed to give the exhibitors feedback for improving their chances of winning the coveted Best of Show prize in future competitions. In Savannah's experience, winning an art competition was pretty much a random chance event. So many of them were either rigged by a "reward my buddies" approach or, worse, a "pay it forward to get favors" approach. The number of competitions that awarded prizes in an ad hoc fashion was also a source of frustration.

Savannah had entered shows only where she was sure to sell her works. That was really the only merited award. Did you reach people strongly enough for them to pull out their wallet and take that piece home? Ultimately, that was the grand prize.

"How's it going?"

Looking up from her clipboard of forms, Savannah was delighted to greet Keith, standing in front of her with his arms folded as if waiting for the answer to a question he had asked in a workshop. She smiled.

"It's wonderful, terrible, exciting, and terrifying. Did I get them all?"

"You might also throw in exhausting, but it's still early."

"I'm too excited to be tired." Savannah took off her hat and drew a hand through her hair. "Yet."

"You certainly look the part of sophisticated business owner judging an art show." He tipped his genuine Panama hat, worn in concert with a Hawaiian shirt along with khaki shorts, and the final touch was Key West Kino sandals. Only the local Floridians would appreciate his authenticity.

Savannah waved a hand from his head to his feet. "You look like an ad for the Key West Chamber of Commerce. I think you've been down there before."

Keith looked down and grinned. "Your artist's eye serves you well. I have a small condo down there that I mostly turn over to a resort to manage for rental. I squeeze in a couple of trips a year during school breaks. I need the occasional top-up in sunshine and I'm not likely to ever get enough sun in Seattle."

"It still appears to be rolling out some excellent glass artists. I've seen the exhibition pieces that your students brought. They are simply amazing. I don't know how I'm going to choose between them."

"I understand, but choose you must." He pressed his lips into a thin line. "It will make an enormous impact on the career of one of them."

Savannah pushed aside a feeling of inadequate

preparation for this job. Why did everything happen at once and only when she wasn't ready?

Keith gripped her arm and looked her square in the eyes. "Savannah, you can do this. Trust yourself."

She smiled tightly. "I'm not sure about that, but you've never been wrong. I'm feeling the pressure of how important this win would be for a struggling artist. I remember what a difference it made to me when I won Best of Show. It was the start of so many good things."

Keith released her arm and smiled. "You've got this. Let's get together tomorrow after the awards ceremony. I really shouldn't be seen fraternizing with the judge."

"Tomorrow seems an eternity away. Thanks, I'll want to dump on someone—it may as well be someone who understands. I'm volunteering at the information booth until four P.M. Sometime after that?"

"Yep, that's good. See you later." He tapped two fingers to the brim of his Panama and strolled away from her.

Savannah adjusted her hat and began the painstaking analysis of the next glass exhibit. She was determined to be a credit to her dad and to Keith.

It took more than three hours to complete the evaluation forms. The professionalism of most exhibits made it challenging to provide useful feedback to the artists, but Savannah was determined to go the extra mile.

Grabbing a quick coffee and pastry, Savannah found a seat in the food court.

"Hey, Madam Judge. Mind if I join you? My feet are killing me."

Savannah looked up to find her office manager standing in front of her table. Amanda Blake was a sizeable young woman topped by yellow and pink spiked hair. She wore an ankle-length native-inspired dress of geometric patterns predominately in pale green and turquoise. Her problem footwear was a pair of too small white beaded moccasins. The crazy combination worked for her.

"Hey, Amanda. Well done—you look amazing. Sit right down. I'm reviewing what I've written for evaluations."

Easing her sturdy bulk into the plastic white chair, Amanda used a neighboring chair to stow her enormous well-used green net shopping bag.

"How are you coping with the judging, Judge?"

"Awesome. The exhibitors are top notch."

"Have you chosen the winner yet?"

"I'm not supposed to talk about this with anyone—you know that."

"Yep, I know that." Amanda smiled with a twinkle in her eye. "Have you?"

Savannah removed her straw hat and tussled her curly black hair. "No. It's frustrating. I'm torn between two artists. They're both so clearly in a category of extreme merit. But I have to choose and it's killing me."

"I know which ones they are." Amanda opened the net bag and pulled out a tightly wrapped burrito, a bag of chips, and a can of Diet Coke.

"Honestly, your curiosity is relentless. I can't talk about this."

"The two booths in the hideaway section near the entrance. Right? Those guys are spectacular, and one of them is a girl. How you are going to choose between them beats the heck out of me," she stated as she wolfed down her burrito.

Savannah felt warmth spread from her chest deep into her heart. *Amanda has not the slightest doubt about my ability to judge these artists.*

"Right now"—Savannah leaned back in her chair—"I don't know either."

Amanda scraped the scraps of her burrito into one last bite and pulled another Diet Coke from the net bag. "So, if I remember right, the plan is to meet you at Webb's tomorrow morning to get ready for Monday's workshop. How long do you think it will take to set things up?"

"Not more than two hours, probably less. I appreciate your help. I don't know what I would do without you."

Amanda launched around the table and folded Savannah into an enormous hug. "You merely have to ask. Compared to my other jobs, this is like getting paid to eat chocolate. I'm loving it, loving it, loving it. Bye now. Good luck with the big choice."

Savannah watched as Amanda trundled across the grass, stopping at a booth every now and again. She left a trail of happy vendors in her wake. Looking down at the stack of papers, she saw that only two remained blank for document-ing her feedback.

Buckle down and get this done.

She gathered up her papers and walked over to the hideaway section and stood in the middle of the aisle. It was now the most crowded part of the show and this section had most certainly been discovered.

Standing off to the side, she was determined to find a difference between the two stars that would decide their fate. The large vessels cre-ated by Leon were resting on tall, rough-cut tree trunk pedestals painted white. The panels of the booth were a light ice blue, allowing his work to stand out against the neutral display.

In dramatic contrast, the inside panels of Megan's booth were covered in long gauze strips of red, orange, and yellow fading up to white. The effect was a riotous movement like a raging fire. Lit from above and below the full-body sculpture seemed to breathe in passionate lust for the fire of life. Keith was right. It was like a flame in the darkness.

Savannah stood quiet and unmoving, letting her curiosity turn her first to the vessels in Leon's booth and then back to Megan's. What could she use to determine the winner? Staring at the fiery torso, she felt the artist's piercing eyes before she saw Megan stalk out to meet her in the aisle.

"Can I help you?" The words were clipped and aggressive.

Megan wore a clinging white cotton dress with Moroccan leather sandals that sported little metal bells that announced each step.

Aware now of how much time she had stood there staring, Savannah spluttered, "Oh, well I was admiring your centerpiece. What was your inspiration?"

Megan's face brightened to the intensity of a desert sun. "Oh"—her face relaxed as she eyed Savannah's clipboard—"you're the judge."

"Yes, I'm Savannah Webb." She fumbled for one of her business cards and handed it to Megan. "Is something wrong? Why are you upset?"

"Another senseless argument with yet another senseless man." She stamped her foot and the bells jingled. "It's nothing. I'm inspired by my passion for the now. I believe that everything I do is embedded in the pieces I create. Since I want those pieces to be incredible, I strive to live a life of excess emotion and expose my senses to wild experiences."

Savannah raised her eyebrows and stepped back a few paces.

"Oh, finding a willing partner is not that hard." Megan looked pointedly at Leon's vessels. "It might be a bit hard on others." She tilted her head in a little shrug. "You know, unbridled passion can be misunderstood for actually caring. It's an unfortunate side effect that when

I'm spent of creative energy, I'm also done with that relationship."

"I think we share a common tutor in our approach to art." Savannah pulled her business card out of Megan's hand and scribbled her cell phone number on the back. "I'd love to have a long chat after this is over. Please call me."

Megan looked at the card, then wrinkled her brow. "I don't think we have much in common at all." She inhaled a quick breath and turned to nearly sprint back to her booth.

"Hey, Megan!" An angry voice boomed across the aisle. "You can't do that! She's a judge." A short, stocky young man who hadn't grown into his ginger beard marched over to Savannah. From her height, she couldn't help but think "teen dwarf," although she did try.

"Not a problem. I'm Savannah." She stretched out her hand.

He shook her hand quickly. "I'm Leon Price. You're not going to let her influence you, are you?" His voice rose an entire octave as it dawned on him that he was making an inappropriate accusation. "Of course not. Sorry." He lowered his head to look at his feet.

"Don't worry. It's the work that counts, isn't it?" Savannah tried to sound calm and judicial.

He looked up at her. "That's hard to remember when everything you want to accomplish swings in the balance." He looked over to Megan's booth with sad eyes. "Everything."

He abruptly did an about-face and went to the back of his booth.

Savannah stood in the middle of the aisle feeling a little abandoned, but determined to do the job that her father would wish her to do. *Go back to what is right.*

The choice of fire over ice finally became clear to Savannah: fire.

Chapter 3

Sunday Morning

Sunday morning dawned gray and overcast, and a rare haze of fog obscured the sunrise over Tampa Bay. The humidity was higher than Savannah could remember for Florida in May. She and her puppy, Rooney, a smoky blue Weimaraner, had finished their morning run around Crescent Lake, and she had guided him through a training session on the mini agility course set up in the backyard.

As a bonding exercise with Rooney, Savannah had joined the local agility club and had signed up for his first competition in a rash act of confidence in his intelligence. The structure of attending the classes was good for both of them, but she had completely underestimated the amount of training it required. Her spirit was willing, and it was keeping her fit but mighty sore. They practiced as often as possible. As a team, they wouldn't fail for lack of trying.

Savannah stood in front of her small closet and deliberated carefully before dressing for the final day of the Spinnaker Art Festival. If she chose something too casual, it might call attention to her youth and inexperience. If she chose something too dressy, it might look pretentious and aloof. Splitting the difference, she wore a tailored black jacket over a plain white cotton blouse, khaki slacks, along with her straw hat and jute shoes. She thought her kiln-fired earrings in black, white, tan, and red with their matching pendant felt exactly right.

The format for presenting the awards hadn't changed a bit since the start of the festival in 1976 as part of the city's bicentennial celebration. The artists were crammed cheek to jowl beneath the dining tent, with extra tables spilling out onto the grass. The food was a feast of pastries sponsored by the downtown hot spot, Cassis Bakery. Egg and vegetable scrambles were supplied by the pub, Moon Under Water, and Mazzarro's Italian Market—Savannah's favorite local roaster—had brought coffee.

The buzz, clatter, and chatter had risen to the decibel level of a high school cafeteria. The hottest topic of conversation was trying to guess who had won the Best of Show award.

Savannah snagged a chocolate croissant and a caffè latte and sat at the judges' table on a raised platform in front of the information tent. The exhibitors were milling around the food court trying not to stare openly at the facedown stack of award certificates—some with checks attached.

Displayed like a rare creature on exhibit, she felt like a fraud. That she could possibly decide their artistic merit was ludicrous. But that was the way of festivals—only the undeserving were rewarded. She determined that she could change that.

Another of the festival judges seated at her table leaned over. "Have you judged before?"

"No. This is my first time. Is it always so nerve-wracking?"

He smiled gently. "Yes, but only if you care."

"Of course I care." She gulped her coffee. "I wouldn't have volunteered otherwise."

Again he smiled. "Good."

The awards ritual involved a period of nervous breakfast nibbling followed by anxious waiting. The waiting stretched the bonds of time until there was almost no time left to finish handing out awards. Then everyone had to run in a panic to set up before the festival opened to the public. The clients who arrived at the artists' booths after the awards ceremony were the customers with money. They bought from the winners. It was crucial to be open for business.

Ugh, frustrating for the artists to be stuck here waiting for the announcements to end.

Although she had a double height advantage with the raised platform and being six feet tall, Savannah couldn't see either Megan or Leon in the waiting crowd. She searched the edge of the food court clearing and saw Leon rounding the corner, coming out from one of the exhibit aisles. He walked-ran and quickly scooted into the group of glass artists who had collected together near the podium to hear the results.

A good bit later than most thought right, the head judge, Elaine Cash, arrived breathless but impeccably dressed in beige summer linen and spectator heels. Savannah had never met her, but now felt justified in taking care with her clothes. Elaine finally stood behind the podium and tapped the mic with her finger. The screeching reverb caused everyone to groan and cover their ears.

"Oh, I'm sorry. Can you hear me?" She carefully pulled the microphone closer to her. "Welcome to the thirty-ninth annual Spinnaker Art Festival. I wish to acknowledge and thank our sponsors for supporting this festival with their time, money, and enthusiasm for this St. Petersburg institution." Looking down at her clipboard, she said, "Please stand up when I call out your organization." Peering over the clipboard with a look that would freeze lava, she added, "Hold all applause until I have finished the list."

The head judge read off about fifteen names of local business organizations, and one by one a representative stood. The crowd remained silent and then she prompted, "Let's give them a rousing round of applause for their unstinting support."

As the enthusiastic applause died, she went on, "Next, I would like to introduce the judges for each entry category in the festival. Judges, please stand and continue standing until I have completed all the introductions. Artists, please hold your applause until I have finished."

Savannah stood when the glass art category judge was announced, and then at the end of the introductions the artists gave the judges a warm and enthusiastic round of applause, mixed with fist pumps, whistles, and woot-woots.

"Now, the part you have been waiting for—the awards." She peeked over the clipboard with a mischievous grin. "We'll start with the individual category awards, followed by the Best of Show award."

The head judge proceeded to announce and hand certificates out to each category winner and then pause as a photographer took a picture of each winner. The categories were arranged alphabetically, so it didn't take long for the glass award to be announced.

Savannah heard the head judge announce to the crowd, "Category prize for glass goes to Leon Price." Leon turned beet red and threw his egg croissant to the ground with a loud, shocking curse. He struggled through the crowd muttering not so much under his breath, "She's done it again. This is not fair. After everything I've suffered, she's done it to me again."

He was a little more under control when he reached the stage and realized that everyone was unusually quiet. He smiled, but not with his eyes.

The head judge handed Leon his certificate along with a nice check for $500. Taking the check, he started to leave, but Elaine was having none of that. She needed to provide fodder for their photographer. Elaine firmly latched onto his elbow so that he posed for the publicity photograph, resulting in Leon looking completely ungrateful for his prize.

As soon as Elaine released his elbow, he scurried off the stage in an ungainly trot.

Savannah sympathized with Leon because clearly he knew that winning the category prize meant that he wouldn't be selected for Best in Show. It was bad form to let the disappointment show. But for Savannah, it meant that her first choice, Megan, was the honored artist who snagged the big prize of $25,000. It truly was a big deal. Savannah grinned like a Cheshire cat.

The head judge continued to award the remaining category certificates and pose for photographs with the same smile and the same stance for each artist. Savannah predicted that the photos were going to look silly and be ridiculed on the social media sites after the event.

Savannah was delighted that the watercolor paintings of Buddha won a prize. She thought they were animated and inspirational beyond their simple form. In any case, in artist time, the handing out of prizes took forever. The crowd was getting restless and checked their watches, concerned about the fast approaching time for opening the festival to paying collectors.

At last, the head judge reached for the final certificate, the check, and the elegant trophy that listed the names of all thirty-eight previous winners on a large brass square. Tapping the mic once more and, of course, acting shocked with the reverb squeal, the head judge cleared her throat. "Now, for the announcement we've all been waiting for. The award certificate, trophy, and twenty-five-thousand-dollar check for Best of Show go to Megan Loyola."

There was a yelp near the edge of the crowd. Savannah turned to see a small woman duck her head and clamp a hand over her mouth.

Then the crowd responded with enthusiastic applause and shouts of congratulations for Megan. Everyone looked around while they were clapping, but no one appeared to be moving aside to clear Megan's way toward the podium.

The head judge pursed her lips into a thin red line, then leaned over the microphone. "Again, Best of Show goes to Megan Loyola. Congratulations, Megan. Come up and get your prize, please."

Savannah scanned the restless crowd as everyone began muttering and looking around. It was clear that no one was claiming the award.

The head judged frowned over her trusty clipboard. "Has anyone seen Megan Loyola this morning? Anyone?"

There was a wave of looking around followed by a rambling grumbling of answers ranging from "No" to "Not me" to "Nope."

The head judge put her hand over the mic and scowled furiously as she mouthed *Where is she?* to Savannah and the rest of the judging panel. The crowd reaction was not only more and more rebellious, but some exhibitors were leaving to ready their booths for the last day of the festival.

Savannah hopped off the platform, then headed over into the maze of festival booths. Some of the artists had sent assistants or partners into the aisles to begin prepping for the opening crowd. With the economy only now recovering from the artist-killing recession, no chances to entice a buyer were being overlooked. This was the last day and the last chance to get rid of those hard-to-maneuver pieces so they wouldn't have to be packed and dragged to the next stop in the art festival circuit.

Savannah asked each vendor if they had seen Megan. No one had seen her since late last night.

She rounded the corner of the hideaway aisle and hurried down to the end booth. Not only was Megan nowhere to be seen, but in the assigned spot where her entire booth and its magnificent masterpiece had been was nothing but a lonely patch of trampled grass.

Chapter 4

Sunday Morning

Savannah's stomach sank, and she was unable to shake the feeling that something was wrong—very wrong. Savannah asked the exhibitors next to Megan's booth if they had seen her tear down and pack up her booth. No one had seen Megan since last night. She continued to ask more artists in the last row, but nothing. It didn't make sense.

Leon's booth was still buttoned up from last night, but there was a great bustling at the booth next to Megan's. A husband and wife pair were unclipping the tarps and cloths that protected their larger pieces of pottery.

She tapped the woman on the shoulder. "Excuse me. Have you seen Megan? Do you know when she packed up?"

The woman turned to Savannah. "That little minx? Good riddance, I say." She bent down to get a box of pottery to unpack for display on their shelves. "Sorry, but I didn't get near her. Excuse me, but we need to get our booth ready."

Savannah smiled and talked to a few of the other bustling artists. None of them could explain why or where Megan had gone.

Ready to give up, she turned to find Leon opening his booth. "Hey, Leon. Do you know what happened to Megan?"

He finished placing one of his vessels on its tree trunk pedestal, precisely centering the artwork. "I haven't a clue." He cleared his throat. "She should be here. This is normally the best sales day." He rubbed the back of his neck, then shrugged his shoulders. "She is a bit crazy."

"So I hear." She pulled out her phone and dialed Keith. "Have you seen Megan? She hasn't shown up to pick up her award."

Sounding like he had been asleep, Keith replied, "What? Who's this?"

"It's Savannah. I'm at the festival. Do you know where Megan is?"

"No, what's the problem?"

"I told you. She didn't pick up her award money. Plus, her booth has been taken down."

"That's strange."

"If she gets in touch with you, have her give me a call."

Savannah ended the call and looked at her watch.

Unfortunately, she was out of time. Each judge traditionally worked at least one volunteer shift at a festival booth. Savannah had chosen the information booth. Not only could she get off her feet, it would also give her a chance to practice talking to strangers about promoting Webb's Glass Shop.

Her volunteer shift started at 10 A.M. and ended at 1 P.M., which left plenty of time after that to meet Amanda at Webb's to help set up for Monday's fused glass workshop. Amanda was planning to help her prepare the kits. She had been taking glass classes at Webb's for years and it had been a good choice to hire her to help manage the enormous backlog of workshops and classes. They were both excited about teaching fused glass as it's a fairly easy skill to learn and the effort would produce artworks that students could hold in their hands quite quickly.

The simple nature of the process was a good return on the investment for business, especially since most students returned to buy glass and rent kiln time for their projects. Webb's Glass Shop had a healthy cash flow, but no small business could afford to be complacent. Savannah had high hopes that this would be a very popular class.

She smiled at the thought because she could hear her dad reminding her that hope was not a plan—a plan was a plan.

She walked over and stood between the two volunteers at the information booth. One was wearing a name tag that declared her to be Wanda Quitman, a long-term organizer who Savannah remembered from her prior years.

The other was a tallish black man, who quickly turned to her with a warm smile and a faintly familiar voice. "Hi, I'm Sam Falco, bartender and aspiring artist."

Savannah scrunched her brows.

Wanda was wearing a white long-sleeve tee under this year's festival shirt. She was perpetually in charge of ensuring that the information booth had a sufficient stock of T-shirts, cups, caps, and tote bags with this year's imprinted design. She was gaunt and heavily tanned, with an animated torrent of chatter. Constantly fussing, folding, and arranging the festival wares, her most useful personality quirk was that she kept a running commentary on all the gossip within the small group of volunteers that kept the festival running smoothly.

"Have you heard about the fiasco at the awards ceremony this morning?"

"I'm one of the judges," admitted Savannah. "I was there on the podium."

"It was shocking to everyone that Megan didn't come up to receive her check."

"Yes, I was—"

"Shocking to the head judge, of course. I don't think anything like this has ever happened." She leaned over to Savannah as if to whisper, but apparently she didn't know the meaning of the word because the volume of her voice didn't change. "They say she has disappeared altogether. What do you think of that?"

Startled, Savannah leaned away and put a

protective hand to her ear. Wanda straightened up and shook her head tsk-tsking like a school-teacher.

"Well, I—" Savannah grabbed her chair and moved it a few inches out of whisper range. She sat and sighed, relishing the delicious comfort of finally sitting.

"It's disgraceful, that's what it is. Simply dis-graceful." The organizer bunny pulled out one of the T-shirts from the XXXL-size stack, re-folded it, and placed it on top of the perfect stack, then moved over to the XXL stack.

Leaping into the chatter gap with her hand held out, Savannah said, "Hi, I'm Savannah Webb. I was one of the judges who nominated Megan for Best of Show."

Wanda stopped her folding and straightened up. "Oh, you're John Webb's daughter, aren't you?" She sidled up to Savannah and reached very high to hug or, more accurately, hang from Savannah's neck. "My name is Wanda, Wanda Quitman. I heard that you would be a judge. I was so sad to hear that your dad had been mur-dered. You were involved with that, weren't you?"

Savannah stepped back a pace. "Not in his murder. I wasn't even here. To be clear, I was lucky to be a help to the police."

"Well, I heard that it was a little more than just luck. Anyway, how did you like being a judge? I heard it was your first time."

"I found it exciting but challenging as well. The works were either excellent or extraordinary.

Nothing in my experience was helpful in choosing between the top two artworks. It was agonizing—especially when so much is at stake."

"How did you finally choose?"

Savannah rubbed the back of her neck and recalled her thoughts in that final selection moment. "It was the strong emotion I experienced when I looked at Megan's exhibit. Her pieces haunted me in a profound metaphysical way—both individually and as a collection. The longer I viewed the installation, the more I felt the fire. Not only fire as an instrument of destruction, but fire as an instrument of rebirth as well. She was the one."

"She certainly sprang out of nowhere."

"Right. But she's a student of one of the finest instructors I've ever known. You're right, though, her rise seems justified for such a unique creative process and for her level of talent. The buzz has come up crazy fast within the industry."

Wanda continued to sort and straighten more shirts and finally worked herself down to the XS stack. "It appears that this spring is her first outing as an exhibition artist."

A harried mother of twin boys in a double stroller that looked larger than Savannah's first car rushed up to the table. Savannah looked up at her blue Hawaiian shirt. "Have you seen my husband? He's wearing the same shirt that we are." She pointed to the little boys, who were wearing miniature Hawaiian shirts.

"No, I haven't," Savannah talked over Wanda's chatter.

"He was getting us some hand-squeezed all-natural lemonade." She spun around and looked to the right and left of the information booth.

"It's right over there behind that clump of palm trees." Savannah leaned over to point toward the far left. "You can barely see the lemon color of the cart."

"Thanks, thanks." She spun the monstrous stroller around while the twins babbled to each other, not the least bothered by the confusion around them.

As Savannah leaned back in her chair, she was welcomed by Wanda's chatter, which had not stopped even while Savannah was helping someone.

". . . scooping up awards all over the South. In fact, she's unstoppable. She's won top awards at every show she's entered."

"Oh, that's unusual," said Savannah.

"Unusual? It's impossible. Even at shows that are historically biased toward their organizers, she's won them flat out and should have quite a nice little bankroll by now."

Wanda continued without a break, "Isn't it strange that she has literally pulled up stakes and left without a word to anyone? I just don't understand why she has disappeared." Wanda stood with her hands on her hips surveying the organized stacks of promotional products for the festival. "I think I had better get down to the children's tent now. They're always in need of some organization. Bye now."

Feeling a bit sorry for the volunteer in charge of the children's tent, she turned back to the bartender and extended her hand. "Hi there. My name is Savannah Webb."

"Hi, again. I thought I was going to have to use dynamite to get a gap in the running deluge of chatter from Wanda."

"Well, I hear she is a tireless organizer and the committee loves her."

"Not everyone loves her. I heard that she and Megan had a very public spat at the Friday night reception. I wasn't surprised that those two big personalities wouldn't see eye to eye."

"Do you know what it was about?"

Sam squinted hard. "I think it was something about her booth." He waved a hand. "A lot of them came in for a drink after the open bar closed. It was insanely noisy."

"I've seen you behind the bar at . . ." She closed her eyes and rubbed her temples with her fingers. "Don't tell me, you just said where. How could I forget?" She opened her eyes bright and said, "Moon Under Water."

"Who hasn't? St. Pete is still a small town—for the locals, anyway."

"It's nice to put a name to the face. A bartender interested in art?"

"Yep, I confess. I'm a stealth artist along with my waitress wife. We've got a booth near the entrance in the miserable hidden aisle. It's doing a booming business now that Megan's disappearance is the source of so much gossip. My wife says we've sold all our small prints and have several corporate clients interested in the large one."

"Have you been exhibitors before?"

"No, this is our first year. I'm jazzed about it because the committee this year raised the quality of the show by throwing out the grandfathered exhibitors and making them submit an application along with everyone else."

"What?"

"Yeah, if you were accepted one year, it was essentially a free pass and a guaranteed entry for all succeeding years. That is, as long as you didn't miss a year. This year was a clean slate. That's why we thought we might have a chance. Some of them were furious. They depended on their sales here to help them survive the slow summer."

"Did you win anything?"

"Yes! We won in our category and took third place overall. That was very exciting. Really, though, getting access to this kind of crowd to show off our work is an extraordinary opportunity by itself. It makes our crazy shifts and crazy hours worth the grief. Say, aren't you the judge for the glass category? I saw you at the awards breakfast."

"Yes." Savannah could predict the next question by now.

"What happened to Megan? Why didn't she collect her prize?"

A couple with an Australian accent interrupted to ask for directions to the nearest loo, and Savannah pointed them to the row of Port-O-Lets next to the seawall.

Turning back to Sam, she replied, "I don't understand. It looks like she left in the middle of the night and took everything with her. Today would have been a big day for sales—especially since she won Best of Show."

"She packed up and left? That's unheard of— she won't be invited back."

Savannah frowned. "I hadn't considered that. Even worse. Honestly, I don't get her behavior at all. Did you see her yesterday?"

"Yeah, she seemed wound up."

"Right." Savannah sat up in her chair. "Other than the fight with Wanda, did anything else happen?"

"Now that you mention it, there was one more thing. She had an argument with some man right before closing."

"Were you close enough to hear it?"

"Everyone along the entire aisle heard it. They were yelling loud enough to wake the dead."

"What about?"

"Whatever it was about was mentioned before the cursing started, and, believe me, that young lady's cursing would make a sailor blush. Anyway, by the time I stepped into the aisle to listen to them, they were well into the name-calling stage, so I have no idea what the argument was all about."

"What happened next?"

"They stopped just short of hitting each other. Fists were actually clenched and drawn. I think that was what seemed to shake them out of themselves. They realized that customers were standing around them gawking. They both froze. Megan went back to her booth and the man walked out of the festival exit gate."

"Do you know the man?"

"Nope, never saw him before."

"What did he look like? Maybe I know him."

"He was a short man with an elaborate comb-over that didn't move in the breeze. That was scary."

"That sounds a lot like Frank Lattimer. He owns the downtown glass studio. He's been a festival committee member for ages."

Is that why she was upset yesterday? Frank can be rudely single-minded when he's trying to make a point. Why would he be arguing with Megan? That's what I would like to know.

Chapter 5

Monday Morning

The sun was softly rising over the rippling waves of Tampa Bay when Savannah and her quickly growing Weimaraner, Rooney, jogged down the sidewalk edging the Coffee Pot Boulevard seawall. It was one of the pleasures of the day for them to get their training run done before Webb's Glass Shop needed to be opened at 10 A.M.

As a high-energy breed, Rooney needed exercise every day that incorporated both physical and mental challenges. In their agility training class for beginners, the instructor had suggested that at least a three-mile run on the day of class would be beneficial for Rooney's attention span. In other words, he was too easily distracted when not tired.

It was a great place to run because the cars along Coffee Pot were unable to go fast over the uneven and occasionally wobbly brick streets.

There was also plenty of warning because the tires made heaps of racket on the road.

Rooney had finally stopped trying to smell every bench, tree, and gate and they had settled into a comfortable jog. He was behaving beautifully, running along on pace with Savannah even with his leash loose. They skirted the municipal pool facility, where early morning swimming practice was in full splash. They passed by the deserted playground. It was too early for the stroller brigade to gather. They approached the lonely tents standing silent and patiently awaiting packers to take them down.

She stopped to take a picture with her phone, thinking it would make a haunting and powerful black-and-white photograph.

When they approached the beige portable trailer that served as the office for the festival committee, Rooney stopped so suddenly in front of Savannah that she tripped over him and landed on her knees in the grass.

"Rooney, what on earth is wrong with you?" She sat up, looked back at him, and was shocked. The hair all along his back was sticking up and he was staring at the trailer with eyes in pointing focus. She followed his gaze, but there was nothing around the trailer. "What is it, boy?" She smoothed down his hair and scratched him behind the ears. Neither of these actions moved him an inch.

"What is it, Rooney?" He sometimes didn't trust her. Rooney had been her father's puppy, and she'd adopted him after her dad's death.

He sometimes regressed into a lonely mood. "Show me, Rooney."

Rooney's toenails scrabbled a running start across the sidewalk then into the grass in front of the trailer. He pulled Savannah around the back and stood looking down into the water from the seawall ledge. He let out a small, throaty whine and then tipped his head back and howled his heart out.

"What is up with you, Rooney?"

She looked down into the water and gasped a silent shriek. Bumping into the rocks below in rhythm with the outgoing tidal wavelets was the body of Megan Loyola.

Her hands flew up and she backed up a step. She pulled at her collar, then covered her mouth to convince the rising bile not to explode. She stood stiff until Rooney's howl registered with her consciousness.

"Rooney, shush now. Quiet, boy. Be quiet." He stopped his mournful yowling.

"Sit. Stay." He sat alert, but his gaze locked onto the wavering body below.

Savannah scrambled down to the small ledge of slippery rocks that were at the base of the seawall and stood there for a moment. It was obvious from the olive putty color of her skin that Megan had been dead for quite some time. Savannah didn't want the tide-driven waves to pull her out into the bay, so she carefully tugged on Megan's cold, wet arm to guide the body up onto the rocks.

Holding on to Megan's sodden sleeve,

Savannah reached into her pocket, pulled out her cell phone, and dialed 911.

"Nine-one-one, what is your emergency?"

A sour taste bulged at the back of her throat interfering with her voice.

"Hello, this is nine-one-one. What is your emergency, please?"

Savannah quickly swallowed. "I've discovered a body floating in Tampa Bay."

"Yes, ma'am. May I have your name and location?"

"My name is Savannah Webb. My location?" She looked around quickly. "I'm standing on the seawall that's part of Vinoy Park. I'm behind the portable trailer that was used for the Spinnaker Art Festival yesterday."

"Please stay on the line until an emergency vehicle reaches you, ma'am."

"Tell them that I'm here with my dog. He's not yet full grown, but very protective. I'm holding on to the body so it won't wash out into the bay. Please hurry."

"We will, ma'am. It should only be a couple of minutes. Just hang on."

Savannah muttered to herself, *I am hanging on, literally.*

Turning a little toward Megan's body, she caught the glint of something embedded in the wet hair on the side of Megan's head. It was a large glass shard. From the vivid orange red, Savannah recognized it and guessed that it had broken off of Megan's exhibit piece. Megan's Best of Show piece had been used to kill her.

Although it was probably only a few minutes, the wait for the emergency vehicle seemed longer than waiting for water to boil in her big red enamel pasta pot. The 911 operator kept telling her that it would be just another minute—every minute. Her arm was beginning to ache, and she was considering whether she should change hands by setting the phone down when she heard the first siren. The emergency medical vehicle ran up the curb, drove onto the grass, and parked beside the trailer.

At the slamming of the doors, Rooney howled like his world was ending. Savannah tried to shush him. "Quiet, Rooney. Lie down. Down, Rooney."

Savannah felt grateful when Rooney stopped, looked at her, and lay down on the seawall beside her. "Good boy," she said, resisting the urge to cuddle him, and put the phone back to her ear. "The EMT is here now, so I'm hanging up. Thank you."

"Yes, ma'am."

Savannah slipped the phone in her back pocket and switched the grip on Megan to her other hand. She shook the numb hand like a rag doll to get back some circulation. Even in that short swap, she felt the tug of the tide. Her grip was the only thing that was preventing Megan from disappearing out into Tampa Bay.

Two emergency responders came over to stand on the edge of the seawall. "Savannah Webb?"

Savannah nodded and peered up at a young man and even younger-looking woman. "It's really slippery down here and the tide is going out. Find something that will keep her from floating away."

"Yes, ma'am. My name is Larry and this is Sheila. I'll be right back."

"That's the fifth time someone has called me 'ma'am' in the last ten minutes." She glared up at the young woman and said through gritted teeth, "Don't even think about calling me anything but Savannah."

"Yes, ma—, Savannah." When Sheila saw Rooney sitting there tilting his head in concert with her movements, the young EMT's eyes widened and she stiffened. "How . . . how beautiful." She cleared her throat. "They said he was a puppy. He's a big puppy—really, really big. Is he yours?"

"Yes, he's still learning his obedience commands. I'm not sure how much longer he's going to be able to hold to his training."

"Will he bite?"

"No, no, he's not aggressive, just very enthusiastic about helping me and he has no clue about how big he is."

The young man came back from the emergency vehicle with a long length of rope. He looked at his partner. "Sheila, stand lookout in case the police squad arrives. Direct them this way so that they can get the coroner down here as soon as practical. Hopefully, we won't get yelled at for touching the body to keep it from drifting away."

"Right." Sheila scooted off to stand on the street side of the truck.

"I'm coming down there now, ma'am."

Savannah rolled her eyes and shook her head slightly.

Larry made a loop at the end of the rope and lay flat on the seawall. "I'm coming down there beside you; then I'll slip this over her arm so you can let go."

"Watch your step, it's deadly—"

She had a blurred vision of big boots and a dark uniform right before she felt a sharp thud against her shoulder. She flew sideways, making a great splash and dragging the sleeve of Megan with her as she tumbled into the water. Bobbing up to the surface, she heard Rooney's panic-stricken howling, then saw a gray streak leaping over the rocks, hitting the surface, and swimming in a straight line for her.

She kicked her feet and felt her hand being pulled down by a great sluggish weight. Looking around, she realized she had somehow traveled a few yards from the seawall and could feel the tug of the tide pulling her and Megan out to the middle of Tampa Bay.

Larry surfaced in a great white swoosh and gasped for air. There was a bloody gash over his eyebrow. Sheila tossed him a life preserver, and he grabbed it before it hit the water.

Rooney was paddling like mad toward her and then she heard a great splash behind her. Looking around, she saw that Sheila had tossed a life preserver circle that had landed over her head barely within reach. Savannah knew she had to get to it before either Megan or Rooney dragged her under again. Slipping her arm around the life preserver, she held on to Megan and pushed the floating circle toward Rooney. His eyes were so wide she thought she could see the wheels in his brain spinning with the thought that he wasn't about to let another human die on him.

Savannah was going to have to make a choice between letting Megan go or helping Rooney. It wasn't really a choice. Rooney was alive. She held on as long as she could, but when Rooney's front paw hit the life preserver, she released her death grip and helped Rooney get into the buoyant ring from the inside. They both dog-paddled to the seawall and pitched up against the slippery rocks.

A second EMT vehicle had pulled up next to the trailer and several hands reached down. "Get Rooney first," she spluttered up at them. "I won't come out until he's safe."

Sheila gently stepped down onto the slimy green rocks and put her hand through Rooney's collar. "I have him, Savannah. Let the officers help you. I've got him."

Confident in the young woman's calm sensibility, Savannah took one of the hands reaching down to her and scrambled up over the seawall and collapsed on her back in the grass coughing. One of the EMTs immediately covered her with a blanket, which she threw off with the next coughing fit. Propped on her elbow, she finally got her breath.

"I'm fine. Larry has hit his head and needs help. Help him first."

"I think you're going to be all right, ma'am. Stay right here for a few minutes." The EMT turned to Sheila and said, "Make sure she's okay." Then he sprinted over to the seawall, where they were trying to get Larry out of the water.

Rooney escaped from Sheila and his front paws threw Savannah back to the ground. He licked her face so furiously she had neither chance nor desire to sit up. After he calmed down a fraction Savannah snuggled him close and sat up to see the second set of EMTs bundling up Larry for his trip to the emergency room. Sheila marched over with her medical kit and knelt in the grass.

"How do you feel, Savannah?" Sheila grinned and scratched Rooney behind the ears. She wrapped a red blanket around Savannah's shivering shoulders. Sheila also used a small towel on Rooney. Of course he adored the rubdown, but as soon as the towel was removed, he shook the extra drips everywhere and plopped onto Savannah.

"I'm fine. Just wet." She struggled to push Rooney off her lap and get up. "I need to get to work."

"You're not going anywhere right now, Savannah," said Detective Parker as he bent down to help pull Savannah upright. "I need a statement from you on what has happened here."

Savannah smiled at the sight of Detective Parker. He had been the investigating detective involved in solving the murder of her father earlier in the year. It was very nice to see a familiar face.

"I told the nine-one-one operator that I found Megan Loyola's body in the bay, and I got down over the seawall to hold her so I could keep her from drifting away."

"Where was this?"

"Over here." Savannah took Rooney by his leash and shifted the blanket tighter around her wet clothing. They walked behind the portable trailer and looked down into the mossy rocks and murky water.

Megan was gone.

Chapter 6

Monday Morning

Savannah spent a little over an hour describing how she found Megan Loyola's body to Detective Parker. He let her leave Vinoy Park, but told her to stop by his office later in the week to sign a formal statement. She scurried home, showered, changed, and took Rooney for a super quick walk before finally heading in to Webb's.

It was going on 9:45 A.M. as Savannah finally parked in one of the owner parking slots in the alley behind the row of business buildings facing the main drag on Central Avenue. Entering through the back door, Savannah tossed her backpack in the oak desk chair and her keys on the worn surface of her dad's ancient rolltop desk. Both had been in the family forever, and she was the fourth generation to use the desk to run a business.

The backpack was a strong reminder of good

times spent exploring nearby parks with her dad. He had insisted that she always carry water, snacks, a first-aid kit, binoculars, and a rain poncho, along with a Swiss army knife in her pocket. That way they could always leave on a moment's notice.

"Hey, Amanda," she squeaked out as she tried to catch her breath while walking through the door into the classroom. "I'm sorry to be late. Something terrible happened on our training run this morning. Did you get my text?"

As the newly appointed office manager of Webb's Glass Shop, Amanda had taken a dress-for-success approach that combined a hint of Goth and *Project Runway*. Confident in her size, she had chosen for today's outfit a bright marine blue silk shirt over black satin jeans with a row of studs down the sides. Her spiked yellow hair had newly dyed tips of the same shade of marine blue. Converse sneakers in teal completed Amanda's look. "You just missed Edward. He left you a coffee and a blueberry scone in the office. I haven't checked my phone. What text?"

"Darn, I wanted to talk to him." Savannah looked around the classroom. Each of the six student workstations had been set up for the workshop with a stack of glass on top of an 8 x 10 brown envelope. The glass pieces were in three colors along with a clear pane of practice glass. "Oh, you've got everything already set out. That's fantastic, Amanda. It looks like we're ready for class. It was great that we prepared everything last night."

"But what did the text say?"

Walking over to the instructor's worktable, she picked up the sample piece and held it up to reflect the light. She put it down as quickly as she noticed that her hands were trembling. It was one of her father's early attempts at fused glass bowls, and she would be devastated if she dropped it. It usually sat on the kitchen counter filled with snack bars, dog treats, and the occasional concert ticket.

Savannah leaned against the worktable and sighed before answering Amanda's question. "On Rooney's training run this morning, he stopped in his tracks along the seawall where the festival's portable trailer was still set up from yesterday. He had sniffed out a body."

"What?" Amanda's eyes widened and her brows dived.

"Yes, and it gets worse. I climbed down to keep it from drifting away and it was Megan, the winner for Best of Show. She didn't arrive for the award ceremony on Sunday morning."

"So, did she fall in somehow?"

"No, there was a shard embedded in the side of her head that looked like it was from the winning artwork in her booth. I can't get my head around so much destruction. A priceless artist is dead, and her priceless piece of art is destroyed."

"Who did it?"

"I have no clue. But that's not even close to the main problem."

"What do you mean?"

"After I called nine-one-one, the EMT fellow knocked me into the water and he hit his head. They took him away to the hospital. He's the only one who saw the body."

"But you had hold of her."

"I had to release Megan to keep Rooney safe. Now she's nowhere to be found, but Detective Parker was at the scene and I have to sign a statement downtown."

"Calm down and don't worry. I'm sure they'll find her, won't they?" Amanda asked while rubbing Savannah's back. "Try not to worry. At least now we know why she didn't show up for the award."

"Larry, the EMT specialist, fell in trying to rescue me and Rooney. I hope his head injury is not too serious, I think he and I are the only ones who have seen Megan's body."

"I can see you're upset, but you didn't know her, did you?"

"Not directly. She was the next star student at Pilchuck after I left. I was on the same track for launching my career." She looked into Amanda's eyes. "If I hadn't left Seattle to run this shop, that body this morning could have been mine. I'd better call Keith. He'll want to know."

Savannah called Keith's cell, but it went straight to voice mail. She left a message to call her as soon as he could.

The old-fashioned hanging bell on the front door of the shop rang to let them know that the students for the workshop were beginning to arrive.

"Already?" Savannah looked at Amanda with a "what gives?" gesture. The first in were the Rosenberg twins, elderly but spry, reliably perennial students. They took every class and workshop offered by Webb's Glass Shop. Today, they dressed in yellow. Canary yellow tops over canary yellow slacks over canary yellow sneakers tied with canary yellow shoelaces.

"Hi, Savannah, we're ready," said Rachel, the eldest twin.

"For your class," said Faith, the younger twin.

"Good morning to you, ladies. You look different. Have you—you're not wearing glasses."

"That's your artist's eye," said Rachel.

"Yes, we both had cataract surgery and we don't need our glasses," said Faith. "Look, I can wear eye shadow now." She batted her eyes like the heroine in a bad silent film.

"That's trashy," said Rachel. "You look like a hoochy mama."

"No, I don't. You're just jealous." Faith posed like a movie star, putting one hand behind her head and the other on her jutting hip.

Savannah struggled to keep a straight face but lost the battle. "What on earth is a hoochy mama?"

"You don't know?" Rachel's mouth dropped open. "Well, it's quite clear that you were raised up without a mother. It's a lady of loose morals, if you know what I mean."

Savannah felt the rush of blood to her temples. "Well, I'm sure neither of you qualify."

"You're wrong again," taunted Faith. "She doesn't know what a hoochy mama is because she *was* raised right."

They went into the classroom and settled themselves in the back row still bickering as they perched on their work stools.

The bell jangled again and a petite woman with closely cropped white hair entered the shop. "Hello? Am I at the right place for the fused glass workshop?"

"Yes, yes, come right in." Savannah extended her hand to a crisp grip. "My name is Savannah Webb. Welcome to Webb's Glass Shop."

"Good morning, I'm Miss Helen Carter and I should be registered."

Checking her name on the list, Savannah replied, "Yes, I have you. Have you taken any art classes?"

"No, Miss Webb. This is my first. I am about to retire and want to explore new ways to fill my time."

"Good, fusing glass is a great way to start. Let me show you through to the classroom." Savannah led Miss Carter into the next room. "This is where we'll work on our fused glass pieces this week."

Miss Carter stood in the doorway and surveyed the room with a critical eye. "Someone who cared about teaching set up this room." She turned to Savannah. "You seem a little young for that kind of wisdom, Miss Webb."

"Please call me Savannah. My dad designed this layout and perfected the class size. He insisted that three rows with only two workstations per row was the optimum size for serious instruction."

"How delightful." Miss Carter selected the first-row seat nearest the whiteboard and instructor worktable. "Is he still teaching?"

"No, he passed away earlier this year. I've taken over the shop."

"Oh, I am sorry. My condolences."

"Thank you, Miss Carter. Settle in and we'll start the class soon." Savannah left the classroom and returned to the display and retail room. She opened her eyes wide to prevent the tears that overtook her calmness. *I still miss him so much, I'm not sure it will ever get better.*

A young couple stood outside on the sidewalk peering up at the store sign, checking the address numbers with a scrap of paper and looking lost. Savannah opened the door. "Are you looking for the art class?"

They looked at each other and in a practiced silence signaled that the girl should speak. "Yes, we're enrolled in the fused glass workshop. Is this the place?" Her voice was soft and round with an unmistakable Canadian accent.

"Yes, it is. You must be Janice and Gary Hill." Savannah held the door open wide and they stepped in. They were dressed alike from head to toe wearing T-shirts from McGill College in Montreal, Canada, with tan safari shorts and bright white sneakers.

What is this dressing alike thing? The twins and now the Canadians? Yikes.

"The classroom is through this door and there should be an empty row available. If you want to sit next to each other, I mean."

They looked at each other, and this time it was the boy's turn. "That will be perfect."

As they were settling into the middle row, the door jangled again. Savannah rushed out to see a young slender man with a long thin pony-tail entering Webb's. "Good morning. Are you Dale Yates?"

"Yes, ma'am. I'm here for the fused glass workshop." Through his thin wire-rim glasses, he had the sensitive look of a misunderstood genius. He looked around calmly at everything in the room but didn't make eye contact with Savannah.

There's that "ma'am" thing again. I need to get more sleep. I must look tired.

She walked to the classroom talking over her shoulder. "The class is about to start. Settle in and we'll begin in a minute."

Dale took the last remaining seat in the front row and Savannah walked over to the instructor's station. On her small worktable, angled to look out at all her students, sat a laptop with a tiny projector no bigger than a deck of cards.

"Good morning. If I haven't already said, my name is Savannah Webb and I am the owner of Webb's Glass Shop. I'm excited to provide this new class. I have two new assistants to help me. The first is my office manager, Amanda Blake."

She waved a hand to Amanda, who had entered the classroom and placed a work stool in the back corner.

"Morning." Amanda nodded and wiggled up on the stool. "Nice to meet you."

"Amanda will soon be teaching classes of her own. My second assistant is some new technology for this class that should help me give better instruction and far more examples of fused glass works than I could hope to provide with in-house pieces. It's a combination laptop, whiteboard, and projector sometimes called a smartboard. We'll have some examples for you to touch and feel as well, but having access to the most popular social media sites is a powerful teaching aid as well."

She picked up a small fused plate that was displayed on a brass stand. "This is what we're going to make this week. It's simple, but we'll learn the most common techniques and skills you'll need for creating fused glass works. Namely, cutting, assembling, firing, coldworking, and a lot of information about the types of glass you'll be using.

"But first, a little housekeeping. Our class this week runs from ten in the morning until one in the afternoon. The restroom is on the left as you go into the office. You need to wear short-sleeved shirts, long slacks, and closed-toe shoes. Make sure they're comfortable. If you have long hair, tie it back.

"No eating or smoking in your work area—there are lead and chemical products here. You are free to bring drinks, but they must have a closed top, as we'll be working around flying shards of glass. All the safety equipment you'll need is furnished. The general format is a short lecture along with a demonstration video. This is followed by a bit of supervised practice. Then you'll create your piece using the skills you've learned. After that we place your work in the kiln and fire it to a high temperature overnight."

A waving yellow arm signaled an urgent question from Rachel. "How many pieces can we make every day?"

"Good question. The limit is one per day per student. We'll be loading up the large kiln with at least six pieces and that will take some pretty creative arranging each night. Any other questions?"

Miss Carter raised her hand in a small, queenly wave. "What if we don't like the colors of our practice piece?"

"It's not a problem if you want to substitute for other colors. Just let Amanda know which colors you want to replace and she'll get you another one. After you have created today's exercise, you get to select your own glass. Is that good for you?"

"Yes, Miss Webb. That's a perfect solution. Thank you."

Savannah rubbed her hands together and looked over the class. "Now, before I go any further, let's get the introductions going. Just your name, occupation, and reason for signing up for this class." She directed her hand to the first row.

Turning slightly to stand beside the work stool, the first student started her introduction. "I'm Miss Carter, language arts teacher from Northwest High School." She looked over the top of her tortoiseshell half-glasses and added, "I prefer to be called Miss Carter, please. I'm retiring very soon and wish to investigate artistic avenues for supplementing my pension." She sat and primly folded her hands.

Remaining seated, the next student said, in a barely audible voice, "Dale Yates. Student at Eckerd College. I'm taking this for course credit."

Savannah looked at the second row and the Canadian man stood up.

"Hello, I'm Gary Hill and this is my sister, Janice. We're Canadians from Three Pines, Quebec. That's about forty miles south of Montreal. We're staying in our parents' condo downtown and wanted to take some art classes while we're here. We're both students at McGill College." He smiled at his sister and sat.

Savannah pointed to the last row in the classroom. The elderly twins wiggled up. In their struggle to rise one of the stools fell over with a huge bang. "Faith, you clumsy old bat, watch what you're doing."

"It was an accident," said Faith on the verge of tears.

"That's what you always say. You have too many accidents," Rachel said.

Amanda hurried over to place the stool upright.

"Hush, hush, ladies. It's no big deal." She hugged Faith. "Not a big deal at all." Amanda moved between the two and put an arm around each. "I'll do this. These cherished ladies are our most loyal clients. They are Faith and Rachel Rosenberg from this neighborhood. They attend every workshop that Webb's Glass Shop offers. It's pretty amazing that they walk from their house every day. Especially when you consider that they are eighty-seven years old."

At that, the class gave them a round of applause. They blushed and found their seats again, basking in the special tribute.

Savannah winked at Amanda and mouthed *Great save* to her.

"Now, let's get going. First, we're going to practice cutting glass on the clear pane that's sitting on top of each stack of glass."

Just as Savannah lifted her sample the front-door bell rang in a customer. She nodded to Amanda to answer it. Amanda returned in barely five seconds.

"Savannah, sorry, but it's Detective Parker. He says he has something for you to sign."

"Thanks. Say, Amanda. You've taken this class—" Amanda nodded like a puppet. Savannah chuckled. "Thanks, please go ahead and start the glass-cutting demonstration. It's the normal beginner's lesson. I'll be right back."

Detective Parker stood tall in the display and retail room of Webb's Glass Shop, slapping his small black notebook against the palm of his other hand. "Good morning, Miss Webb. I'm on my way back to the station, and before I have your statement typed up for signature, I need to confirm a few more details."

"No problem. How can I help?" Savannah frowned at the cool greeting and stiff posture. *Why is he being so formal?*

"It's a coincidence that I can't ignore." He stopped tapping the notebook.

"What is?"

"You were one of the last people to be seen with Megan at the festival on Saturday afternoon."

"I was? I didn't know that."

"You were also the one to discover her body." The notebook slapping resumed. "Statistically, that doubles the probability that you killed her. Plus, we found your business card in her pocket with your personal cell phone number scribbled on the back."

A cold sweat broke out at the top of Savannah's scalp and raced down the back of her neck. "You found her?"

"Yes, not long after you left."

"But, you must know that I wouldn't have killed her. I have no motive."

"Means and opportunity weigh more than motive in an investigation." He lowered his voice. "Motive usually strengthens an effective prosecution, but it's not a deal breaker for making an arrest. As long as the evidence supports the suspect's actions, we'll go forward."

Savannah pressed her lips tight to hold back the indignation that rose in her throat. "You can't seriously support that view."

"I know what kind of person you are, Miss Webb, but statistics and process must be taken seriously."

"But this is just—"

"We don't have the resources to investigate lines of inquiry that have little chance of payoff. You are a suspect for Megan's death."

"This is just insane."

"Miss Webb, please make this easy for all of us. Do you have an alibi for Saturday night after midnight?"

She scraped a hand through her hair. "No. I was home alone with Rooney. I was exhausted after judging the festival." Her fingers began to tingle, so she rubbed them. "I went to bed early because I needed to be back at the festival for the artists' breakfast and awards ceremony. I didn't know Megan was missing until Sunday morning."

He slipped his notebook into his inside suit pocket. "Your formal statement will be ready to sign in a few days. I'll call when it's ready to sign."

He shook his head slightly and gave her a weary half smile. "Do us both a tremendous favor—get yourself off the list of possible suspects as quickly as you can."

Chapter 7

Stunned by Detective Parker's declaration that she was a suspect, Savannah watched him leave and then turned around toward the classroom. She didn't think she could talk coherently, let alone teach at the moment, so she poked her head into the classroom and signaled for Amanda to carry on and then ducked into the custom workshop that opened off of the display and retail room.

It was quiet and still. She made her way over to her late father's workbench and sat. She flipped the light switch over the bench and looked over his tools. She skimmed her fingers over the fragments of cathedral glass that he had been working on at the time of his death.

Although a few months had gone by since her father's death, she still wasn't ready to clear off his workstation. There was plenty of unused work surface in the room to work on the shop's commissioned pieces. She wouldn't clear off his bench yet. Not until she was ready.

What would he think of this situation?

Taking in a deep breath and exhaling long, Savannah struggled to predict his advice. He wouldn't want her to risk her safety, but he also wouldn't want her to waste her skills in a critical situation. He *also* hadn't been particularly trusting of the police, in life or in death.

What would he want me to do?

He would want her to investigate Megan's murder to clear herself and preserve the reputation of Webb's Glass Shop.

She had carried out an investigation before to find the murderer of her father and his master craftsman. She could do it again. Especially if she convinced her friends to help her one more time. With an impending murder charge hanging over her head, it wouldn't take much to reassemble the posse to gather the kind of insider information about the local glass art scene that the police department wouldn't know to ask about.

"Thanks, Dad," she whispered.

Flipping off the workbench light, she turned to the door and found her apprentice Jacob Underwood standing beside her with his beagle service dog, Suzy, in his arms.

"Who are you talking to?"

"Sorry, Jacob. I was mostly talking to myself." She reached out with both hands and nuzzled Suzy's long floppy ears. "Hello, little sweetie." Looking at Jacob's lowered head, she followed his gaze to Suzy's paws. "Oh my goodness, what perfect little booties. Does she like wearing them?"

"Not very much."

"Well, it means she can stay with you in the shop no matter where you go. We don't have to be worried about broken glass on the floor."

"She's a good little dog." Jacob spoke with his chin resting on Suzy's head. "I think she tolerates them only because she understands that they mean she can stay with me."

"This is much better than making her stay in my office at the back. This is a good thing for us all. Did you come up with the idea?"

He shook his head. "Nope, my mom did."

Savannah smiled. "Well, then please thank your mother for the terrific solution."

"Yes, Miss Savannah."

And now you can be calm in here while you work instead of checking on Suzy in her basket back in my office every five seconds.

She watched Jacob set Suzy on the floor.

Suzy stood on four stiff legs and looked up at Jacob, tilting her head as if to question his judgment for making her wear these foolish things. As soon as Jacob started for his workstation at the far end of the custom workshop, Suzy gave a vigorous shake and carefully goose-stepped her way to his chair, where she sat and looked up at him in her "on-watch" pose.

Savannah poked her head into the classroom to ensure that Amanda was doing fine. Then she pulled out her cell and dialed Keith.

He answered, "Hi, Savannah, what's up?"

"Oh, Keith, something horrible has happened to Megan. I found her body drifting in Tampa Bay this morning. She'd been hit in the head by her centerpiece." She took a calming breath to ward off the sobbing she felt building in her chest. "I'm so sorry. She was apparently killed Saturday night."

"I don't understand. This is terrible. Who did it?"

"The police don't know, and right now, they're inclined to think that I did it."

"What? That's ridiculous. Has anyone notified her parents?"

"I don't know. I imagine they've contacted the Seattle Police Department by now and have sent someone to do that."

"I'll call Leon and Vincent to let them know. As far as I know, Leon was her most recent boyfriend. I'm not sure if they were still together. She tended to jettison her partners right before a major exhibit. Is there anything I can do?"

"I don't know—this has knocked me sideways." She took a deep breath. "I'll be fine."

"Seriously, Savannah. If I can do anything—anything—you must call," said Keith.

"Thanks, I'll let you know."

Savannah made her way back to the classroom and stood to the side until Amanda finished her demonstration of glass cutting.

"Amanda, that was very well presented. I appreciate your willingness to take over. Class, I apologize for the disruption, but you are always in good hands with Amanda."

Amanda flushed from the top of her blouse to the broad smile plastered on her face.

"Now, let's move on to the next skill."

For a terrifying moment, Savannah's mind went blank. She couldn't remember the next teaching point.

If Detective Parker is giving me a warning, I'm in deep trouble.

She walked over to the instructor's workstation at the front of the room and looked down at her teaching plan for the day. Thank goodness for a written plan. She sighed softly and her shoulders relaxed.

"Next, we're going to cover some important numbers that get a little technical, but, I promise, not too scary. The trick here is that you want your pieces to fuse together safely in the kiln. If the glass is incompatible, the pieces will heat up and cool at different rates. Depending on the design of your work, you risk cracking or even shattering the piece when it cools. Amanda has an example of a beautiful platter that basically exploded during the cooling cycle."

In a large clear plastic storage bin were the pieces of an intricate platter. As she handed the bin to Miss Carter, Amanda said, "It's absolutely heartbreaking. There were six different pieces of art glass in the platter."

"What you're looking at"—Savannah paused to make sure each student was looking at her—"was my first attempt at a complicated fusing. I had breezed through the beginner pieces and gotten cocky." She waved a hand at the bin. "This is the result of my overconfidence."

The bin slowly traveled around the classroom, causing a few frowns and murmurs of sympathy. Savannah reached beneath the podium and drew out a presentation box. She removed a beautiful platter. "This is what my second attempt looks like."

The class expressed a collective "awwww" as she held the beautiful platter up for them to admire.

While the finished piece made the rounds, Savannah went on, "I painfully learned the value of checking the type of glass I was fusing after having to collect the shards of my first platter out of the kiln. As a result of the accident, I had to meticulously examine each kiln surface to ensure that none of the shattered fragments remained behind to cause further contamination with new works."

Amanda collected both the plastic bin and the finished platter from the Rosenberg twins. Faith said, "I'll bet your dad was angry."

"Oddly, no, he wasn't angry. He was frustratingly patient. His main concern centered on the kiln. It was the only kiln we had at the time, so production ground to a halt right in the middle of a commissioned project of plates for a new restaurant. I spent two days taking it apart, cleaning it, and reassembling it under his eagle eye. That part was not pleasant. Our profits took a big hit that week."

Miss Carter raised her hand halfway in a small wave. "How do we avoid this?"

"As I said earlier, simple care and attention. The science of glass fusing is built around a number called the Coefficient of Expansion. It's commonly referred to and pronounced as the C-O-E. The value is usually expressed as a whole number. The glass on your tables comes from the Bullseye Company and they specialize in a COE of 90, so artists"—she looked pointedly around the room—"and that includes each of you . . ."

She waited for the compliment to reach their eyes and was pleased to see a few smiles.

". . . artists simply refer to it as COE90 glass. Spectrum, another common glass manufacturer, has a COE of 96, while Corning's Pyrex glassware has a 32 COE. Standard window glass, referred to as 'float' glass by the glassmaking community, has a COE that is usually around 84 to 87, while Moretti glass, commonly used for lampworking, has a 104 COE."

"Yikes!" said Dale. "That's a lot to remember. How do I know what I have?"

"Good question." Savannah picked up a small piece of glass. She pointed to a label in the corner. "This is what comes on the sheet when I receive it from the manufacturer. It clearly indicates that the COE of this sheet is 96. As I cut each sheet for sale or for use in a project, I write its manufacturer's stock number and the COE on both of the cut pieces."

"You've done that for our glass." Dale held up one of his glass pieces.

"Yes, and it's something you should make a habit of doing as soon as you cut your glass for a project."

Up came Miss Carter's hand. "But what about the small pieces? That seems terribly tedious."

"Good point. For my small pieces, say about three inches square or less, I put them in a plastic bin clearly labeled COE96. For our creation today, and for the rest of the week, we'll be working in COE96. That way, you have no chance to make a mistake."

"What about getting more glass after class is over?"

"Out in the display and retail room, the racks of glass are separated into two large areas. On the right side of the door is stained glass and on the left side is glass for fusing. The fused glass is separated into the two most popular ones: COE90 and COE96. There are large signs over the racks. If you want to get more glass for this week's workshop, make sure you select it from the COE96 rack."

Looking up from his notebook, Dale said, "Thanks, that helps a lot. I don't want to spend two days cleaning up the kiln."

Everyone laughed.

Savannah held up a small oblong platter with a chevron design. "This will be our project for today. You have enough glass on your workstations to create this and, of course, you'll want to save your scraps. There are about a dozen similarly sized molds right up here for you to choose from. Let's get creative."

A scraping of chairs signaled the release of the students.

"I want the smallest one. I need a little soap dish for my bathroom sink," Rachel said as she snatched a small curved mold. "Faith, there's another one just like it."

"I don't want to make what you're making. I'm going to make a bowl." Faith picked up a mold and they made their way to the back row.

"Do you want to make something for our folks?" Janice looked at Gary. "The condo doesn't have many serving dishes."

"Great idea. How about these two platters?" Gary pointed to two long narrow molds. "If we use different patterns but out of the same colors, they'll look cool."

Miss Carter walked up to Savannah. "Do I have to use a mold? I would like to try something a little more free-form."

"Of course you can. Use the surface of your work area as your base. First, you need to lay down a sheet of kiln paper, and then you build your design. After you glue it together, we'll transfer it to the kiln and it will get fired along with everyone else's piece," said Savannah.

Amanda walked up to Dale, who was madly scribbling away in his notebook. She tapped him on the shoulder. "Are you going to select a mold? I can help you if you need some ideas."

He looked up into Amanda's eyes. "Uh, sure, y-yes, sure, I'd l-l-like some help."

Winking at Savannah, Amanda led Dale to the collection of molds. Each mold had a finished piece placed on top to use as inspiration. Wrenching his eyes from Amanda, he scanned the molds and said, "Which one is your favorite?"

"Oh, that's easy. This one." She lifted a circular bowl with a simple two-color star design. "It reminds me of my gran. She was always admiring the stars and showing me the constellations in the night sky."

"Then, that's my choice." Dale picked up the mold and returned to his workstation.

Savannah nodded to the group. "Now that everyone has a mold, it's time to prepare your glass. Start by cutting your glass to fit the mold. Amanda and I will answer any questions you might have. Just call us. We'll be in the display and retail room." She motioned for Amanda to follow her out of the classroom.

"What is it?" Amanda whispered loudly. "You've been acting strange all morning."

"Not really surprising when you consider that Rooney and I found Megan's body on our run this morning."

"I know. I can't stop thinking about it either." Amanda sucked in a quick breath. "Not really the best way to start the day."

"It's even worse. Detective Parker hinted that I was their prime suspect." Savannah wandered over to the sales PC and slumped down on the stool behind the counter.

"What? That's ridiculous!"

"He really shouldn't have told me. But I think

he did only because of my prior work on Dad's case. He told me to get it in gear and clear myself before he had to take action."

"What are you going to do?"

"First, I'm going to ask Keith to help. He knew her very well as her mentor and might have some ideas about why she has been killed. He has to know something that will give us some leads."

"Then what?"

"I want to investigate Megan's death. I also want you and Edward to help."

Amanda clapped her hands in a flutter and whistled. "So, you're getting the band back together?"

Savannah rolled her eyes. "You are determined to find the bright side of anything, aren't you?"

"Yep, it's my thing. How soon do you want to start?"

"Right away. Jacob is already here. He's so off-the-charts creative. His perspective is an advantage in any problem-solving discussion." She pressed her lips thin. "Would you please call Edward while I finish the class?" Savannah stood, put her hands in the small of her back, and stretched her stiff neck from side to side.

As if he had heard the conversation, Jacob stood in the office doorway.

"I can be a big help." Jacob moved beside Savannah with Suzy in his arms. "I was able to solve some big clues last time. You know I'm good with patterns and puzzles. Patterns that you didn't see."

Savannah looked at Amanda. "That's right, we can use that."

Jacob stood taller. "I could analyze all the data right here in the shop. That wouldn't interfere with my routine or alarm my mother."

"He's got a point," Amanda said. "Here in the shop would be fine."

"Okay, but you simply must get permission to do this from your mother. Our last case was somewhat unplanned. We're doing this one deliberately. If she's fine, I'm fine. Agreed?"

Jacob nodded. "Mom will agree."

"Let's meet here after class, say at four this afternoon. We'll come up with a plan and re-assemble our posse."

"I don't understand," Amanda said. "How could Detective Parker possibly think you could murder Megan? He knows you."

"Yes, and I don't think he believes that I killed her. But I knew her, I discovered the body, and then they found my business card in her pocket with my personal cell number on the back."

"Why did you give her your card?" Amanda asked.

Savannah paused and stared at the floor. "I wanted to find out what my life would have been like if I had continued with my studies in Seattle. She practically stepped right into my old life with my scholarship, my instructors, and even my dreams. I wanted to know her better."

Amanda nodded. "Unfortunately, your curiosity now has you tied to her murder."

Chapter 8

Monday Afternoon

Sitting around in various chairs in the small back office of Webb's Glass Shop, Amanda, Jacob, Edward, and Savannah nibbled on the batch of cinnamon scones that Edward had brought from his pub. Memories of their previous investigation flooded Savannah. It had been a struggle to connect with her dad's community as the new owner of Webb's Glass Shop, but afterward, she'd appreciated their unstinted support.

"What's this about?" Edward spoke between bites of his scone. "More promotional ideas? Queen's Head is frantic! We're not only getting ready for the Grand Central Chili Cook-off but we're extending our breakfast offering to weekdays. Did you know that Nicole is not only a great bartender, but used to be a short-order cook?"

"No, she never mentioned it. She's going to tackle that?"

"Yes, indeed, on Friday after she returns from

visiting her sister in Switzerland. She and her partner are saving for a house. The extra dosh will help with the down payment. Are you planning a way to add early morning classes?"

"Nope, not yet. I'm busy training Rooney in the mornings."

"Just tell them, for Pete's sake," insisted Amanda. She puffed out her cheeks. "It's a murder."

Jacob piped up, "I'm going to help with data analysis."

"Murder? What murder?" Edward stood up tall and his green eyes narrowed.

Savannah stood and paced in front of them. "Please, guys, let me tell this in my own way. Sit down, Edward." She stood silent until he was back on the stool. "When I judged the glass category at the Spinnaker Art Festival this weekend, my first place selection also won Best of Show."

"Too right. The festival was covered in the *Tampa Bay Times* Sunday paper. It was a huge success. No mention of a murder," said Edward.

"That's because it hadn't been discovered." Savannah paused. "Yet."

"Yet?" Edward stood and folded his arms across his broad chest. "Come on, Savannah. Out with it."

"Okay, okay. Hold your horses. The artist that I chose, Megan Loyola, didn't show up to the awards ceremony to collect her twenty-five-thousand-dollar check. When I went to check her booth, it had been cleared out and there was no sign of her."

"What happened?" Edward asked.

"When Rooney and I were on our training run this morning, we found Megan's body in the water behind the festival's portable office trailer."

Jacob looked at Edward and Amanda. "Miss Savannah talked to Mr. Webb's worktable this morning. That usually means she's upset."

"Yes, I'm even more disturbed now that Detective Parker has informed me that I'm the prime suspect for her murder."

Edward moved over to Savannah and quietly folded her into his arms.

She nearly melted in warmth. He was so closely tuned to her feelings.

He whispered into her curls, "How is that even possible? Has the world gone berserk?" He kissed her cheek.

Savannah gently escaped out of Edward's arms and looked into his worried eyes. "It's because I was one of the last few people to be seen in public with Megan and I'm also the one who found her body. Detective Parker came by this morning and gave me an unofficial warning that I was under heavy suspicion."

"I still don't understand how he can think that." Amanda sighed deeply. "He knows you're a good person."

"Logically, I completely agree with Detective Parker's reasoning. I'm the most rational suspect at the moment, but that should change." Savannah broke away from Edward and looked at the three one by one. "The trick is going to be to help him find the real killer before Detective Parker has no other choice but to arrest me."

"If we're going to find another killer"—Jacob looked down at the floor—"we need another plan."

"You've hit the nail right on the head." Amanda polished off the last bite of her scone and brushed the crumbs off her ample chest. "Let's get cracking and find Megan's killer."

Edward spread his hands wide. "But, where do we start? We don't know anything."

"We actually each know a lot"—Savannah folded her arms in front of her chest—"but we don't know it as a group. I have an idea. We need to do what Detective Parker does for each case. He has a murder room where all the evidence and information is posted on a wall. I saw it during the investigation of my dad's case. Let's do the same." She stepped up to the whiteboard on the wall opposite the old desk and picked up the black dry-erase eraser.

She hesitated. The sketches and notes written there were her father's and she hadn't wanted to use the whiteboard. It gave her a comforting feeling that he was looking over her shoulder as she struggled with the finances and piles of paperwork the business generated.

She turned to the wall beside the desk that had a corkboard crowded with mandatory employment posters, Grand Central District newsletters, business receipts, scraps of preliminary sketches, and, oddly, a striped sock. "We could clear this off and—"

Jacob stood in front of the whiteboard. "This

is the best method. It'll help everyone to know what's happening."

Dad wouldn't hesitate, and neither should I.

"You are absolutely right." In broad, sweeping strokes, she quickly wiped everything from the whiteboard and wrote "The Case of Megan Loyola's Murder" across the top of the board.

"There's one suspect we know." She wrote "Suspect" at the top-left corner of the white-board, then drew a vertical line down to the very bottom. She then wrote "Investigation" to the right and drew a horizontal line under both words. "He was seen arguing with Megan late Saturday afternoon." She wrote "Frank Lattimer" and then noted "Subject of argument at Festival" beside his name and drew a line beneath both across the whiteboard.

"Really?" Amanda said. "That slimy shyster. He's always smack-dab in the middle of every-thing trying to get more students for his classes. Does anyone know what the argument was about?"

Savannah turned her back to the whiteboard. "No, but that's one thing we can investigate. At the very least he could be a good lead. That's something I can do. He's always running into the shop to snoop into my business."

Jacob put his hand up. "Miss Savannah, the kind of glassworks that Megan created needs a team of helpers. Who are the helpers?"

"Yes, indeed. Her pieces were enormous and would have required a team of two, possibly even three, to create." She turned and wrote "Megan's team" on the whiteboard along with "Identify" in the next column. Turning back around, she asked, "Who wants to track down her production team?"

"Me, me, me." Amanda gave her best imitation of an excited schoolgirl. "I can do that. Do you know where she worked?"

"It has to be the Duncan McCloud Gallery. It's the only hot glass shop in the area with equipment large enough for her works. The studio is about six or eight blocks south of here on Twenty-Second Street."

"Okay." Savannah turned back to the whiteboard. "There are still some others." She added "Wanda Quitman" to the list of suspects and wrote "Upset Megan at reception" in the next column. "I talked to Wanda, or, more accurately, Wanda chattered like a magpie to me during the festival. She was friendly to me, but I think you had better tackle this one." She pointed her marker directly at the center of Edward's broad chest. "I suspect she's a man's woman."

Edward lifted his head and smiled. "What about the site of the festival? Could there be something there that only a glass artist would know?"

"Right on point." Savannah nodded. "Okay, Edward and I will search the festival park right after this meeting." She wrote "Festival Grounds" followed by "Search for evidence" in the next row. "I really need to deflect their focus from me to the real culprit."

"What about me?" Jacob looked at each of

them. "I'm a good investigator. I was very good with solving the puzzles in the last investigation."

"That's absolutely true." Savannah nodded. "There's another category of suspects that I know you will be able to help us with. The other exhibitors in the festival each had to fill out an extensive application form for entry into the award competition. I need your special pattern recognition skills to find connections between any of the other exhibitors and Megan. You are the only one who can do this."

She turned back to the whiteboard and wrote "Registration forms" in the Suspect column and "Find connection patterns in application database" in the Investigation column.

Jacob nodded slightly. "That's good. I can do that."

"I know you prefer paper, so before they remove my access to the exhibitor's database, I'll have all the applications printed out for you."

"Print them in color, please. I want them in color."

Color? Really?

"Certainly, Jacob. I'll have them to you later this afternoon. I'm going to send the database out for Kinko's to print and bind for you."

Jacob's eyes gleamed and he stood an eighteen-year-old's style of tall—which is only slightly slumped rather than completely slumped. "Yes, each application in a separate binding."

That's going to be expensive, but if something is to be found, Jacob is the only one who can find it.

"I called Keith this morning. He hadn't heard about Megan. He mentioned Leon Price as an ex-boyfriend. I'm going to ask him some questions."

"Who? Keith?" Edward asked.

"No, I'm going to ask Leon for anything that could give us some leads." She wrote "Leon Price" and "Megan's ex-boyfriend" in the last row.

"Thanks, everyone. That's an impressive list." Savannah stood and looked at each of them. "I appreciate your help." She rubbed the corner of her eye and blinked rapidly. "Now, let's get to the park so I can have something useful to report to Detective Parker. He's been even grumpier than usual. I think it's because of Officer Boulli."

They all nodded their remembrance of the burly policeman who seemed much more interested in protecting his questionable reputation than solving crimes. In the end, he wasn't successful with either.

Jacob spoke their thoughts. "I thought he was fired. Why is he back?"

Savannah sighed deeply. "I heard that he avoided a dismissal again through a technicality in one of the regulations. It's Boulli's most advanced skill. He was suspended for a few weeks. At least I hope its Boulli and not me that's turned Parker into an ogre."

"You go, girl." Amanda scooted down off her stool. "I'll get everything ready for class tomorrow and lock up the shop. Don't worry about Webb's."

Savannah looked at the whiteboard and nodded approval.

The Case of Megan Loyola's Murder

Suspect	Investigation
Frank Lattimer	Subject of argument at festival
Megan's team	Identify
Wanda Quitman	Upset Megan at reception
Festival grounds	Search for evidence
Registration forms	Find connection patterns in application database
Leon Price	Megan's ex-boyfriend

Savannah quickly downloaded the Spinnaker Art Festival database and arranged to have it printed and bound for Jacob. She grabbed her backpack and keys from the office and waved to Amanda as she and Edward slipped out the back door.

As she settled behind the driver's seat, a cold shiver danced across her skin and sank into her solar plexus.

They drove downtown and parked on the street near the plain tan portable mobile home that served as the festival office. Walking over to the drooping remnants of police crime scene tape, Savannah pointed to the section of the seawall. "That's where Rooney and I found Megan on our training run this morning. It really freaked him out."

"Only Rooney?"

"No, not just Rooney. It truly freaked me out as well."

Edward planted his hands on his hips and turned around looking over the ground where the festival had taken place. "It's still a bit messy, isn't it?"

Savannah smiled at the scattered bits of litter that looked like a ghostly imprint of the festival. "That's going to be to our advantage. I'm sure that the forensic specialists were told to search the area where Megan's booth was set up, but they might not have known how much of the area actually belonged to her. The area behind the booth is what the artists use as a sort of back stage. It's probable that Megan spent a lot of time back there. Let's have a look."

As they walked up toward the part of Vinoy Park that held the artists' booths, Edward pulled Savannah into a side hug. "You're really worried, aren't you?"

Relishing the warm sensation of being tucked into his arm, she said, "I'm very worried. I have no alibi and I don't know what Detective Parker has for evidence other than the business card. I walked everywhere and touched everything as I was judging the artists. It's unnerving."

"We'll solve this—we have before and we'll do it again."

Savannah looked up into his confident face. "I hope so."

They walked in lockstep until they reached the north end of the park. Savannah slipped out of Edward's arm. "This is the general area where Megan's booth was installed. It was at the end of the row about here." She pointed to a flattened square of grass.

"Describe her booth for me. This looks like there was a floor."

"It was a fantastic display representing the power and beauty of fire. I remember there was a rug that was black at the edges that had ever-smaller circles of the colors of fire, from bright red to orange, burgundy, and even electric blue. It was such a simple but effective method for grounding the exhibit."

"Hey, what's this?" Edward bent down and reached for something. "Ouch!" He drew his hand back and examined his forefinger. "I'm cut. Blimey, what was that?" He pulled out his handkerchief and wrapped it around the finger applying pressure on it by squeezing it with his other hand. Savannah looked down at the grass. There were long, slender shards of orange red glass hiding among the blades of grass directly beyond the beaten-down patch.

Bending down, Savannah looked at the pieces. "I was sure there must be something left behind after her booth was packed up. They look like the shard that was embedded in Megan's head wound. Although I didn't get a very good look at her before everything went haywire."

"So, they could be part of the murder weapon." Edward squeezed his finger harder and grimaced at the sharp pain. "Or are they remnants of a dropped work of art?"

"In either case, we need to take these away. Obviously, they're quite dangerous. Kids run barefoot through this park all the time." She reached into her backpack and got one of Rooney's doggy duty bags and carefully slipped the shards into the flimsy bag.

"What if they're evidence?"

"They *are* evidence. We've already spoiled them. You've got blood on them and I've handled them. As the prime suspect trying to clear herself, I'm going to use them for our investigation. Then as soon as we've had a look, I'm going to turn them over to Detective Parker. If we hadn't come to the park to search, they would never have been found. If I get yelled at for knowing a little more than the police about glass, so be it."

She stood. "Here, let's see that." She unwrapped the soaked handkerchief and looked at a deep, narrow cut. "It's a clean cut and the bleeding has stopped, but it needs stitches."

"Stitches?" Edward's face turned pale green. "I'm not good with needles."

Savannah raised her eyebrows. "You're afraid of needles?" She folded the handkerchief over to a clean patch and rewrapped the cut. "Nothing to it. There's a walk-in clinic on our way back. It shouldn't take too long."

"But—"

She stopped his protest with a kiss, then said,

"I'll be right there to hold your good hand. Let's go."

After dropping Edward off at Queen's Head with two tiny stitches covered by a butterfly bandage, Savannah collected the bound applications and dropped them off at Webb's. By the time she drove home and picked up Rooney, they were a few minutes late to their agility class. It wasn't a crowded class, as Monday evenings seemed to be unpopular.

Savannah appreciated the extra attention that Rooney received from their instructor, Linda. His first agility meet was on Saturday, and as a team they didn't exactly shine. Well, honestly, they were dreadful, but Rooney was so keen and enthusiastic, it was a joy just to watch him run.

"Are you ready, Rooney?" Linda knelt to cup his chin and scratched his broad chest. "He looks good. Have fun you guys." She turned her attention to class and outlined the warm-up exercises.

After several sessions of running laps followed by practicing basic commands, they settled into the first lesson of the evening.

While they were running laps, Linda had taken two objects from the back of her Honda Element. The first looked like a low coffee table and the second was a long strip of plywood with poles attached at intervals.

"Calm down, Rooney," Savannah whispered.

He knew that the equipment meant running fun and he wanted to start right now.

"Today's practice will concentrate on learning how to weave quickly through a set of posts. We'll start the dogs on the pause platform exactly like a competition. Then you'll command him to run the weave and return to the pause platform."

She stood on top of the platform. "For those of you who are beginners, this is a slalom. The weave is a series of five to twelve upright poles, each about three feet tall and spaced about twenty-four inches apart. The dog must always enter with the first pole to his left, and must not skip poles. For most dogs, weave poles are one of the most difficult obstacles."

But for Rooney, because he was Rooney, it was simply puppy play. As expected, he had the most difficulty when required to remain calm and still on the pause platform.

Still, they had a lot of fun and were delightfully tired when they arrived home. Unfortunately, no amount of agility practice would make Savannah tired enough to forget about finding Megan's killer.

Chapter 9

Detective Parker sat at his tidy desk with a single folder open in front of him. It was the preliminary results of the autopsy on Megan Loyola. The sections meaningful to an active investigation had been filled in with all other entries labeled "TBD" for "to be determined." The two details that bothered him were the cause of death and the time of death. Although the victim had suffered a crushing blow to the head, the ultimate cause of death was listed as drowning.

"You asked for me?" A large head appeared around the door to Parker's new office. A step up from his former partitioned cubicle, this office featured solid walls and a door that could actually be closed for privacy. Parker's superior officer had designated it to him based on his case closure rate—the highest in Pinellas County. Although he hadn't yet personalized the freshly plastered walls, Parker loved this tiny office.

"No, Officer Boulli, I didn't ask for you specifically. You were assigned to me. That's quite a difference, wouldn't you agree?"

"Oh, I—okay."

The large, bulky man edged around the door and managed to sit in the chair across from the desk without getting very close to Detective Parker. Then Boulli inched the chair back until it touched the wall. It was a feat in studied motion. "What can I do for you, sir?"

"Given our history, I thought it would be good to have a chat before we started to work together again." Parker felt sorry for the straining buttons on the front of Officer Boulli's uniform shirt. Could they be dangerous projectiles? Shaking his head to clear his mind, he added, "Do you agree?"

"Yes, sir." Officer Boulli straightened up slightly and placed a hand on each knee.

"I know we have had some differences in the interpretation of Code of Conduct for a Police Officer as published by the county of Pinellas and the city of St. Petersburg. In fact, our interpretation differences resulted in your suspension of duty after the murders that occurred at Webb's Glass Shop."

"Yes, sir."

"So that we are clear, I wanted you to know that my professional recommendation was that you be dismissed from your position and not permitted to return."

Why does this man bring out the worst in me? His innate incompetence nearly got Savannah killed a few months ago. I need to handle this carefully.

"No, sir." Officer Boulli wiped his sweaty palms along the tops of his thighs, leaving a faint streak on his uniform trousers. "I didn't know that, sir."

Staring at the stain, Parker attempted to relax his jaw. "That's why I'm addressing this issue now, before we continue working together. I expect you to perform your duties with all due consideration of the Code of Conduct and Internal Operational Procedures as they are written as of this date."

"Yes, sir."

"What I mean is that I'm willing to start with a clean slate if you are." Detective Parker leaned forward and folded his hands. "Repeat that for me, officer. I want to be sure that you understand my concern."

"Sir, you are telling me to watch my step."

"Good. Tell me what happens if I file another complaint against you."

"Sir, you won't have to do that. I'm going to be very careful to toe the line."

"But since you are on probation, I want to know if you understand the consequences of another complaint."

"Yes, sir. According to procedure, if you file another complaint, I will be removed from duty until an investigation is carried out by Internal Affairs. If they find the complaint valid, I will be dismissed from employment with the City of St. Petersburg Police Department."

Leaning back, Parker said, "Very good, officer. We understand each other?"

"Clear as crystal, sir."

From the right pocket of his jacket, Parker pulled out a notebook and nodded to Officer Boulli to do the same. "I have a line of investigation for you to follow in the case of Megan Loyola."

Officer Boulli opened his notebook on his knee and patted his pockets searching for his pen. His eyes grew wider as the search grew longer. He stood up to put his hand fully into each pocket and came up empty.

"Sorry, sir. Can I borrow a pen?"

"Of course, officer." Parker pulled open the center drawer of his desk and tossed a cheap stick pen to Boulli. "I want you to start gathering statements from each artist who had a booth in the same row with Megan." He pulled out a yellow sticky pad from the center drawer and copied down a name and address from his notebook. "Here"—he peeled off the top sticky note—"this is the name, address, and cell number of the organizer for the Spinnaker Art Festival."

Boulli took the sticky note and carefully stuck it in his notebook. "Yes, sir."

"Find each artist. Interview them in such detail that I get a clear picture of Megan's movements from Friday night through Saturday night. It's important to be accurate with the times that each artist had any contact with Megan. We need to build a timeline for her movements during the Spinnaker Art Festival."

"Yes, sir."

"Aren't you going to write that down?"

"No, sir. I'm clear about my assignment."

"Very well. Call me every hour on the hour to report your progress. Is that clear?"

"Yes, sir."

Detective Parker stood up and waved a hand to the door. "Well, get going, then."

Officer Boulli stood so quickly the notebook slipped off his knee and fell under the desk. "Shoot. Oh, sorry, sir." He scrunched his bulk down to peer under the desk. "Sir, it's right by your foot. Would you mind?" he wheezed.

Pressing his lips tightly together, Parker stepped back and moved his office chair out of the way. The notebook had fallen open and he could see the illegible scribbles and notes. Picking it up and handing it over, he stared directly at Boulli with cold eyes. "Not an especially good start."

"Yes, sir." Boulli took the notebook and disappeared like a schoolboy on the last day of school, leaving behind a breath of fresh air.

Detective Parker sat down and slowly lowered his forehead to the top of his desk.

"What's wrong?"

Looking up at Forensic Specialist Sandra Grey, he grinned sheepishly. Her skirted suit accentuated her slim, athletic build. "I've just spent the last five minutes being a bully. I'm a hypocrite—a card-carrying hypocrite."

"That's impossible." She sat down and crossed her shapely legs, showcasing a pair of black patent peep-toe high heels. "You are one of the kindest detectives I know. And I should know. I deal with the entire lot of you nearly every day. What gives?"

"I had a discussion with Officer Boulli and I came down on him like a ton of bricks. I don't think it was particularly effective, and I believe I'm the only one in the conversation who will be affected by my rant."

"I'm sure it wasn't as bad as you think."

"Oh, I'm sure it was, but on the other hand, I'm confident that Officer Boulli will be left completely unfazed."

They looked at each other for a silent second, then both burst into uncontrolled laughter.

Sandra recovered first. "Honestly"—she caught her breath—"you couldn't have picked anyone more perfect to bully. He is so concerned with himself, it simply doesn't register."

Detective Parker removed a white handkerchief from his pocket and wiped the tears from his eyes. "I hope you're right, but it's a good lesson for me to stop trying to be what I'm not." He stowed the handkerchief back in his pocket. "Thanks for the best laugh of the day, but besides cheering me up, why are you here?"

"First"—she glanced at the folder on his desk—"I wanted to be sure you had the preliminary autopsy report. They get lost occasionally.

Second, I wanted to confirm drinks downtown at The Canopy at six. Third, and most interesting, I've been examining the glass shard that was embedded in the victim's wound. I'm not an expert on art glass, but this fragment seems quite unique."

He smiled with his eyes. "Canopy confirmed." Then a crinkle appeared between his brows. "How are they unique?"

"Well, they're curiously luminous without adding what I can only call 'shiny bits' to the composition."

"Okay, how does that help?"

"I think this is a new or relatively rare process in glassmaking that could be a driving motive for Megan Loyola's murder. But I can't find anything on the Internet about glass like this."

"So, you're saying that we need expert consultation?"

"Yes, we do." Sandra rose and poked a finger into Detective Parker's chest. "I think Savannah Webb would be very helpful as that expert."

"Before we get ahead of ourselves, let's go over to the murder room."

They walked across the open seating area of the St. Petersburg Police Department's Crimes Against Persons Unit and entered the first conference room in a bank of conference rooms. Along the back wall was a sliding panel system of corkboards flanking a whiteboard in the center of the room. The corkboards were peppered with bits of paper reports, photographs of the scene, and a snapshot of the victim.

The whiteboard took center stage and was customized for the transient nature of fast-moving investigations. Across the top of the whiteboard were the magnetic labels SUSPECT, ASSIGNMENT, and INVESTIGATOR. The first name under the Suspect column was "Savannah Webb" and under the Assignment column was written "discovered body—judge at festival—needs alibi." Finally, listed under the Investigator column Detective Parker had written his own name.

Detective Parker stood feeling a flush creep into his face. He pointed to Savannah's name. "I would sign her up instantly except for the very annoying fact that she is our top person of interest."

Sandra tilted her head. "You know that's ridiculous."

"Yes, but until she is eliminated from the investigation, I can't use her as a consultant."

"What are you doing to clear Savannah?"

"Following other leads." He grinned. "I think she'll manage to clear herself. Unfortunately, not quick enough to serve as an expert consultant, but facts are facts."

"Yes, but—"

He held up his hand and ticked off his fingers one by one. "One, she discovered the body. Two, she was one of the last known individuals to talk to Megan. Three, Savannah chose Megan to win the top prize. Four, her business card was found on the body. Five, she has no alibi. I have to follow the case leads no matter where they take me. In the meantime, I've found another local expert we can use."

"Oh, who is it?"

"He has a glass shop in the downtown area: Frank Lattimer."

Chapter 10

Opening up the back door of Webb's Glass Shop, Savannah could tell that someone was already there. The office's overhead lights were flipped on. It couldn't have been Amanda; she would have turned on the classroom lights as well. Savannah gently placed her backpack and keys on the desk and walked into the dark classroom.

She turned on the lights as she went from the classroom into the display and retail room. Beside the front door was a comfy dog basket filled with Suzy, Jacob's beagle service dog, wearing her blue vest, matching booties, and eyes bright in welcome. The door to the custom workshop stood wide open and Savannah let out the deep breath that she didn't know she was holding.

Of course, it's Jacob.

Walking into the custom workshop, she found Jacob circling the large workshop table stacked

with the Spinnaker Art Festival artist applications.
He was sorting them into perfectly aligned piles.

"Good morning, Jacob."

He lifted his head and nodded slightly, not
missing a beat in his sorting.

"Any news?"

He shook his head no and continued sorting.

"Good luck, then."

She left him to his sorting process. Jacob had
an affinity for recognizing patterns in disparate
bits of data. If anything could be gleaned from
the applicant database about Megan's death,
Jacob was going to isolate that data.

She rubbed the back of her neck to loosen
the knot of tension. *I'm jumpy because of Megan, but
there really isn't any reason for me to be spooked.* This
wasn't like last time, when employees at Webb's
were killed.

Returning to the office, she yawned and
reached into her backpack and took out the
small shards she and Edward had collected from
the grass behind Megan's exhibit space. Taking
them back into the custom workshop, she turned
on the light table and placed the shards on the
bright white surface. Lit from underneath, the
shards looked like glistening bits of fire. They
were even more luminous than when Savannah
had seen them in Megan's central glass figure.

She grabbed a magnifying glass and looked
closer at the shards. The glass looked different,
but she didn't know why. After several more minutes of close examination, there was nothing more

for her to do. She wrapped up the shards and returned them to her backpack.

I need to have Keith look at these.

Since Amanda had closed the shop last night, Savannah didn't expect her until right before the start of the workshop at ten. She returned to the display and retail room, quickly stepping through the opening-of-the-shop routine. Savannah was pleased to see Edward coming through the front door with a French press, cups, and a pile of cranberry scones.

"Hey, luv. Hungry?"

"Yes, as a matter of fact. I'm more interested in coffee, but those scones smell delicious."

"Good. Back in the office?"

"Do you want to share some with Jacob?" She glanced at the opening of the custom workshop.

"You know his food issues."

"Of course, nothing with berries, which, oddly, includes raisins; I forgot for a second. Sometimes my Southern Lady training works on autopilot."

"I thought your mother died when you were only ten. Who gave you Southern Lady training?"

She tilted her head and grinned. "See, you don't know everything. I spent summer vacations with my mother's parents in Kentucky. Gran and Gramps owned a small horse farm near Lexington. She taught me how to cook, how to sew, and how to flirt. Gramps taught me how to fish and how to ride a horse. It was wonderful. I don't think I could have survived without them."

"So, they're gone now?"

"Oh no, they're still up in Lexington. They don't travel much anymore, but I usually spend some time with them in the summer each year. I'll be doing more of that now that I'm living in the same time zone. In fact, I think there's a direct flight from Tampa."

"I know a bit about horses. I learned to ride when I was about six."

"Something else we have in common." Savannah smiled, then frowned. "Did you get in touch with Wanda?"

"Yeah, it wasn't hard. I approached her about being an organizer over the food vendors for next year's Grand Central Chili Cook-off. We're meeting for drinks tonight at the Birchwood rooftop lounge downtown. Remind me again of what I'm trying to get out of her?"

"It's there on the whiteboard." She pointed to the third line. "See, you need to investigate 'upset Megan at reception.'" Savannah frowned. "I think we should add a column for assignments, don't you?"

"Brilliant." Edward nodded.

She stood and said, "Done," then added an "Assigned To" column to the whiteboard. She wrote in who was investigating in each line.

"Yes, I seem to have Swiss cheese for memory these days." He stood close behind Savannah until she felt his presence and turned around. He smiled and looked down into her eyes. "I think I know why."

Savannah cleared her throat. "I don't know what you're talking about. Anyway, this makes it

easier for us to keep track of the investigation."
She finished filling out the assignments and
placed the marker back on the whiteboard shelf.

"What about the shards we found behind
Megan's booth?" Edward pointed to the entry.

"Good point." Savannah wiped out "Festival
grounds" and replaced it with "Glass shards," then
wiped out "Search for evidence" and replaced
that with "Identify origin."

Edward took the eraser out of her hand and
removed his name from the "Glass shards" row.
"I'm sorry, but I really can't help you with that one."

"Okay, fair enough. Are we all good?" She stood
back and folded her arms, looking at the grid
quite satisfied.

The Case of Megan Loyola's Murder

Suspect	Investigation	Assigned To
Frank Lattimer	Subject of argument at festival	Savannah
Megan's team	Identify	Amanda
Wanda Quitman	Upset Megan at reception	Edward
Glass shards	Identify Origin	Savannah
Registration forms	Find connection patterns in application database	Jacob
Leon Price	Megan's ex-boyfriend	Savannah

The front-door bell jangled madly as Amanda bustled into the shop. "I'm sorry to be so late." She hurried into the classroom and then stood in the doorway to the office. "Did you check to see if I have all the materials the students will need for today's class? Oh, hi, Edward. Are those your cranberry scones?" She wedged between Edward and Savannah to snatch a scone from the tray. "Oh my goodness, thanks. These are my absolute, all-time, until-the-end-of-the-world favorite scones."

Savannah winked a "later" at Edward.

"I haven't checked the classroom yet. We were about ready to talk about the investigation. How did you get on with Duncan McCloud Gallery?"

"Super! The managing director, Duncan McCloud himself, was working with three helpers. They were creating one of Duncan's signature large etched vessels and it was a treat to watch the team coordinate their tasks. Unfortunately, the vessel got just a wee bit unbalanced and it broke into a million shards."

"Ouch, that is a heartbreaking sound." Savannah recalled that sickening feeling when the same thing happened to her while developing vital skills in hot glass.

"Yeah, they were upset. McCloud was great, though. He just laughed and said they would try again after everyone rested a bit."

Savannah grabbed the French press cafetière and poured more coffee into her cup and Edward's, too. "What about Megan's production team?"

"Yep, I got the names of her team from the team that McCloud is currently using. Apparently they're the best ones around. Even better, one of them was standing there as part of McCloud's crew."

"That's great. What luck!"

"Yeah, it's luck all right, but not great news. The one who was there was Vincent O'Neil. He was working with McCloud the night Megan was killed."

"Was there another assistant? It was a complicated piece."

"That's where the good luck comes in. The other team member is Leon Price. He wasn't at McCloud's Saturday night with the others. They complained that it was a very difficult shift without him."

"That name is appearing with scary frequency," said Savannah, scrubbing her forehead with her knuckles. "He was the artist that I was debating awarding first place to, but I went along with Megan. Their booths were directly across the aisle from each other. He was also late to the festival on Sunday morning. As her ex-boyfriend and rival, we need to focus on him. Great job, Amanda."

"Thanks, boss. I thought you might want to do that." She handed Savannah a small slip of paper. "I copied his address from McCloud's contact list. He didn't have any information on Vincent."

Savannah looked at the slip. It was an address

in a neighborhood of small studio motels north of downtown. "Great. I'll talk to him when we finish class." She tucked the address into her pocket. "Are you ready to check the kiln?"

"Nope. I want you with me when I open the kiln." Amanda looked at a puzzled Edward. "If one of their pieces is broken, major student disaster." She waved her hands like a muppet. "First, I'll double-check today's materials." Amanda left toward the classroom.

Edward watched her leave and gave Savannah a quick hug. "Let's get together after I talk to Leon and compare notes," said Savannah. "Maybe Jacob will have news by then."

Edward gathered up the cups and tray and left the shop with a bright, "Cheers, then."

Looking at the whiteboard, Savannah erased the words in Amanda's row and wrote in "Vincent O'Neil, Megan's team member, and Savannah" into the empty spaces. She stood there for a long moment, then walked into the classroom and smiled wide at Amanda. "The setup is perfect, absolutely perfect. You'll soon be teaching this class." She moved among the worktables and each station had another small stack of glass squares placed on top of today's fused glass pattern. "Okay, time to face the music. Let's see how yesterday's pieces fared in the kiln."

They went into the custom workshop and opened the large kiln lid to reveal six finished works.

"Oh," Amanda cooed, "they're lovely. Not

one of them broken." She clapped her hands together like a small child being told she could have cake.

"It just gets better and better." Savannah patted Amanda on the back. "This is definitely your medium."

Savannah lifted her chin. *She's going to be a wonderful teacher.*

"Should I take them out and clean them up?"

"No, that's part of the learning process for this first fusing lesson." Savannah and Amanda lifted each piece from the kiln and placed them on each student's workbench.

Savannah said, "Today we'll teach them about kiln paper and cleaning their pieces after they've been fired. If you're careless with either of those steps"—she clapped her hands sharply—"shards."

The front-door bell jangled. "The students are here. That's the start of the day."

The second day of class started with a rush to see how the students' first fused glass pieces turned out.

"This looks awful," Miss Carter cried. "What's all this powdery stuff all over it?"

"Bleh, you can't even tell what color it is." Faith leaned over to Rachel and said, "At least yours looks as bad as mine."

"Patience, patience," said Savannah. "Let me explain what has happened." Lifting up Miss Carter's fused piece, she went on, "This is part of the process when using a kiln. As Amanda loaded the kiln, she used support blocks, dam strips, and lots of kiln paper to prevent each piece from sticking to the bottom of the kiln or fusing into each other. Right, Amanda?"

From the back of the room, Amanda replied, "Yep, it's a bit like loading the dishwasher, except that you have to remember that everything melts. You have to leave room for that."

"Thanks. Now, let's learn how to clean this." Savannah led the way into the industrial sink in the back office and held Miss Carter's chalky piece under the running water and scrubbed it with a plastic scouring pad. "Now, it's ready to dry with one of the T-shirt rags in this basket." She chose one and quickly buffed away the water. "Look how lovely."

"It is lovely." Miss Carter took possession of her artwork. "Thank you," she said with a nod.

Savannah backed away from the sink. "It's all yours now. Please remember that it's glass and can break. There are a few rubber bumpers in the sink, but if you drop it, well, it's gone."

After a critique session that covered the cleaned pieces, Savannah and Amanda led the class through the proper use of kiln paper, tips for loading the kiln, and preparing to fuse a second piece. The time evaporated, and before she knew it they all had their work in the kiln and were busying themselves packing up their tools and waving good-bye.

"If you're okay with buttoning things up and preparing for tomorrow, I'm going to see if

I can track down Leon for a little chat," said Savannah.

"No worries, I can do everything but start the kiln." Amanda put her hands on her hips. "I'll leave that for you."

It took less than ten minutes to find Leon's studio, but she spent another ten minutes finding a place to park. The place hadn't been painted in quite a few years and the landscaping suffered from neglect. There was a rickety black and yellow bicycle chained to a metal support column right beside the studio door.

She knocked on the door and waited for about ten seconds, then knocked again. After another ten seconds, she rapped sharply on the door. "Leon. This is Savannah Webb. Please answer—I'm not going away. I want to talk to you about Megan."

The door cracked a couple of inches and she could see Leon beyond the latch chain. "Why are you here? I don't want to talk about Megan."

Savannah slipped her foot into the door crack. "I found her body, Leon. The police are investigating me. I need to know more about her. Please let me in. It will only take a few minutes. I know you have to go to work soon. I'll stay out here until you do. You know she's been killed, don't you?"

The eyes beyond the chain squinted and blinked for a second. "Yes. I know. Keith called to tell me." There was a long pause. "Move your foot and I'll come out."

Savannah moved her foot and backed up. Leon came outside to stand beside his bicycle. "What do you want to know?"

"Did you see anything suspicious going on with Megan at the festival on Saturday?"

"Nope."

"Keith Irving says that you were involved in a relationship with Megan before the festival. Is that true?"

A rosy flush spread over Leon's face and then turned dark. "She was using me. Apparently it's what she does to charge up her creative juices. We broke up."

"When?"

"Before the festival—right after she finished the centerpiece."

"Do you know if she was in a relationship with someone else?"

"I think she was, but I don't know who. I don't want to know. Is that all?"

"Have the police asked you about Megan yet?"

"No, why?"

"They'll want to know where you were on Saturday night. You know, for an alibi. Do you have one?"

"Sure, I was working with the hot glass team at Duncan McCloud Gallery. I was there practically all night."

"That's a bald-faced lie! Duncan McCloud said that you didn't show up at all that night."

Her response was met with Leon slamming the door in her face. Even after knocking and calling his name, Leon refused to respond or open the door again.

No sooner had Savannah gone back to the office to check e-mail when the front-door bell jangled and she could hear Edward telling Amanda, "Time for tea and talk."

He placed a tray on the side table in the office. "Where's Jacob?"

Amanda silently pointed a "one moment" and fetched Jacob from the custom workshop.

As soon as Jacob found a stool to sit on, Edward handed him a mug. "It's your favorite. Hot chocolate made with almond milk with a vegan gingersnap to accompany it. I've got sweet peppermint tea for us. It's a good match with the regular gingerbread muffins."

"Mmmmmm, this is fabulous." Amanda smacked her lips. "You must keep that baker of yours happy. You must. He's the real secret behind the success of Queen's Head."

"Yes, that and an enormous amount of work." Edward perched on a stool, and Amanda settled into the side chair next to Savannah's antique rolltop desk.

Ignoring the squeak from her matching antique oak chair, Savannah asked, "Let's figure out where we are in the investigation. Edward, you've got your meeting with Wanda?"

"Right, originally I was going to meet her tonight, but she called and now we're meeting for coffee at the Museum of Fine Arts Tea Shop.

She's very busy, or so she said. But it seemed to me that she was very busy telling me how busy she was, but still found time to meet me for coffee on literally no notice."

"Amanda?"

"Nothing new for me."

"Of course, we just finished class. Jacob, have you found anything in the records?"

"I'm finding many things. There are 2,053 applications for the Spinnaker Art Festival. The farthest applicant is from Sydney, Australia, and the nearest applicant is only blocks away from us. She is a student at the Diazzo Warehouse in the next block. Eight hundred twenty-nine applicants are from Florida and a further 317 are from Georgia. Of the remaining 907 applications, 723 are spread across the United States, and the remaining 184 applicants are from the Caribbean, South America, Mexico, and Canada."

"Thanks," Savannah said slowly, "but I'm not exactly sure how that helps us."

"Almost half of the applications are from Florida, but when I compare it to the number of applications approved, there were only ten percent actually able to enter the Spinnaker Art Festival. That's not right."

"That does seems low"—Amanda frowned— "but I still don't see how that gets us anywhere."

"Wait, wait," Savannah said. "One of the volunteers at the information booth was telling me about an issue with the applications this year." She frowned in concentration.

"Well?" Edward reached into the tray for another scone.

"He said that there was a change in the entry rules for returning exhibitors. They eliminated the guaranteed entry for artists who had been granted booths year after year as long as they didn't skip a year. Instead, they needed to reapply, just like any other applicant. He said that there were a lot of longtime exhibitors who didn't make the selection and there were quite a few very angry artists. Some of them depended on the sales of this show to get them through the long, slow Florida summer. It gets too hot for outdoor festivals."

Amanda sat straight up. "So one of them took it out on the new kid on the block?"

Jacob nodded, "I created a list of the artists most likely to be angry about their loss of sales. They're weighted by priority and probability of alternate income sources." He handed her a page of notebook paper with seven names listed.

Shaking her head slowly, Savannah looked at the names. "That seems pretty far-fetched. Regardless, it's an anomaly and that's what we have asked Jacob to find. Good job!" Savannah smiled. "Right. What else?"

"I've compared Megan Loyola's application to other successful applications and hers is quite different. It is very short. The average length of the applications is six pages, with an average of five photographs of art. The specified maximum was ten photographs, not including the three photographs required of the entrant's exhibition booth. Megan attached one photograph of her art and one photograph of her booth. She left most of the application blank."

"That *is* unusual," said Savannah. "I was obsessed with maximizing any opportunity to convince the selection committee that I was a worthy exhibitor. I always submitted the maximum number of photographs permitted."

"But she was selected anyway. Can we see her application?" Amanda asked.

Jacob nodded. "I have it here. It is the shortest one of the 2,053 entries."

"Let me take a look." Savannah reached for it. She flipped through the slim document. "There's hardly any information here at all. No address, no artist's vision paragraph, no gallery references—it's bare bones. The picture isn't even of the red torso, this is a variation in blue. The only means of contacting her is a local cell phone." She flipped another page. "Here's something interesting. Her only personal reference is my former professor, Keith Irving." She looked up at the others. "What could this mean?"

"Who was on the selection committee?" asked Amanda.

"I don't know, but I can find out," Savannah said. "I've been invited to a party-type meeting to discuss any issues that came up from the festival. It's called a lessons learned meeting. All the organizers, judges, sponsors, donors, and some of the award winners will be there. It's being held at the St. Petersburg Yacht Club tonight."

"That's a partying bunch, these Spinnaker folk," said Edward. "Good idea."

"Edward, I talked to Leon Price after lunch. He had the booth across from Megan and he was the runner-up contestant. I asked if he saw anything at the Spinnaker Art Festival that would be helpful. He said, 'Nope,' and he also said he was working at McCloud's on Saturday night with a hot glass team. When I told him that Duncan McCloud said he wasn't there, he slammed the door shut in my face and refused to talk to me." She chewed at the corner of her mouth. "I also still need to talk to the vile Frank Lattimer and find out what he and Megan were shouting about." She stared at the list and the assignments, absently twirling the marker.

"What about the shards of glass we found?" Edward took the marker from Savannah and pointed to her name. "Maybe your mentor would be able to help."

"Possibly, I've looked at them with my magnifying glasses but maybe Keith can suggest something after he's studied them." She took the marker back from Edward, wiped out her name and assigned the shards task to Keith.

"We're making progress, but nothing solid enough to report to Detective Parker."

Chapter 11

Tuesday Evening

The site of the Spinnaker Art Festival "lessons learned" party seemed odd to Savannah. Most festivals carried a bohemian spirit more aligned with an artist's colony; the city's fanciest private club was a new experience.

She parked her Mini at a meter across the street from the St. Petersburg Yacht Club and walked into the street-side entrance. A smiling man dressed in a full tuxedo with white gloves directed her to a reception room filled with elegantly dressed members of the Spinnaker Art Festival. The room shouldered a nautical theme with great dignity bolstered by a navy carpet so thick her kitten heels sank into the pile.

At least I changed into my little black dress and dug out Mom's pearls. I hope this is appropriate.

She hadn't stepped two feet into the room when Wanda swooped over to grasp both hands and give air kisses near each ear. "Welcome,

welcome, Savannah. I'm so pleased that you made it. I know your appointment as a judge was so late that you didn't get to participate much in the social side of the Spinnaker Art Festival. I did remind the committee that it was supremely late for a new person to join our little society, but they were adamant that we needed new blood. I personally prefer the old blood."

As Savannah eyed the beautifully dressed group, it was obvious that all the movers and shakers felt the need to be there. "I didn't realize there was a social side."

"Oh my, my, my, yes, there is." Wanda looked her up and down. "Goodness me, I haven't seen plain pearls in quite some time. You're going to need to go shopping if you want to be a mover in this circle." She hooked her arm into Savannah's and led her into the beautiful reception room.

Savannah looked over at her with undisguised irritation.

"You must meet everyone. Oh"—Wanda cupped a hand around her mouth into Savannah's ear without lowering her voice—"here's the most eligible bachelor in the city. He's an orthopedic specialist, well, really, he does knees and hips. It's a huge practice."

Savannah shook her head in confusion. *Does this woman not understand the mechanics of a whisper?*

Looking at it from a different perspective, Savannah wondered if maybe she had a hearing loss or an aural-processing condition of some sort.

Wanda tapped a tall man on the shoulder. He turned to reveal an expensive navy blazer with gleaming gold buttons, a white open-collar oxford shirt, and a glass of champagne in his bronzed grip. "Dr. Ross Wilkinson, may I introduce Miss Savannah Webb." Savannah cringed at the exaggerated emphasis on "Miss." "Miss Webb stepped in at the last minute to judge the glass category after the tragic death of her father. You remember John Webb, the owner of Webb's Glass Shop down in the Grand Central District?"

Dr. Wilkinson smiled a dentist's dream of perfect porcelain and shook Savannah's hand. "Wanda, where have you been hiding this beauty?" He lifted Savannah's hand up and kissed it like a royal-bred prince. "I am delighted to meet you."

Yikes, what planet are these people from?

"I haven't been hiding her, dear. This is her first social with us. Be nice."

"Of course, of course." He tucked Savannah's hand through his arm and led her to the bar. "I assume you love champagne. I've never met a beauty who didn't."

"Goodness, Dr. Wilkinson, I'm—"

"Please, all my friends call me Dr. Ross."

Savannah clenched her teeth to hold back a cutting remark. But oddly, he was right—she did love champagne and the price was right. She smiled her southern-girl best. "You are perfectly right, Dr. Ross. I would love a glass."

"Good choice." He patted the hand he'd

slipped through his arm. "Let me introduce you to our little group."

"Thank you, I would like to meet the members of the selection committee. They were brilliant in choosing the entrants for this year's Spinnaker Art Festival. I would like to congratulate them personally."

"Very good. I can see that you have some experience working an event. Good choice for making connections that will pay off quickly."

He led her to the full-length-window side of the room that overlooked the shimmering waters of Tampa Bay. A circled group of three men were holding iced amber drinks. They were quietly discussing an issue and completely oblivious of their surroundings. Dr. Ross walked up and cleared his throat. "Excuse me, gentlemen. I am very pleased to introduce Miss Savannah Webb, our newest Spinnaker Art Festival recruit. She judged the glass art category."

The three men turned and the largest raised his glass in salute. "Savannah, what a pleasure to find you here."

Of course Frank would be here.

"Hi, Frank, it's good to see you." She raised her champagne flute.

Frank held his salute a little longer and looked at the other two committee members. "Guys, this is one smart little lady. So, you need to watch out for her. She's the single most dangerous competitor to Lattimer's Glass Shop."

Dr. Ross cleared his throat again. "Yes, yes, Miss Webb, may I present the members of the selection committee. Obviously, you know Frank. This is Lesley Thackson." Dr. Ross indicated a short, white-haired man who was a round, jolly but tanned Santa lookalike. "He is the exhibit director at the Museum of Fine Arts. Lastly, this is Wilson Barnes." This gentleman was of average height, but skinny as flint. "He is the curator of the collection at the Dali Museum."

They each nodded a welcome.

"Gentlemen"—he patted the hand tucked in his arm again—"we need to make John's daughter feel at home."

Lesley extended his hand. "Miss Webb, may I offer my condolences on the tragic loss of your father."

Savannah used this opportunity to extract her tucked hand from the surgeon's clutches. "Yes, thank you." She shook his hand and moved two steps away from Dr. Ross, neatly avoiding a reclaiming.

Lesley kindly looked into her eyes. "He was an enormous influence in our organization. We miss his wisdom and especially his unique skill in keeping such a diverse and often fractious group focused on the goal."

"Such kind words. Did you know him well?"

"We were partner combatants in a shared vision for the Spinnaker Art Festival."

Wilson edged in. "Let me also tell you how glad I am to meet John's daughter. He spoke of your progress in Seattle often. I had a great respect for his experience, but, unfortunately, I usually ended up on the opposite side of any of his Spinnaker Art Festival issues."

Stepping closer into the threesome's circle, Savannah tentatively offered, "I heard that this year's selection committee had changed one of their long-established policies."

"Oh, you mean about the grandfathered exhibitors?" Lesley looked down into his drink. "That was certainly the controversial issue of the year." He gave his whiskey a gentle swirl followed by a long sip. "It split the organization right down the middle."

"Why?"

Wilson looked at the other two and exhaled a double-cheeked puff. "Many of the long-term organizers were convinced that we needed to protect the artists who had been exhibiting for years. They feared that the Spinnaker Art Festival would lose its unique Florida character."

"Was that true?"

Frank laughed an unmanly cackle. "That's where the joke is on us old-timers. It turned out that the local artisans were very well represented and the whole Spinnaker Art Festival stepped up in quality, originality, and even diversity among the artists. Attendance increased by about twenty-five percent. It was a resounding success."

Savannah swirled the remaining bit of champagne in her glass. "How did you select the final artists?"

"It wasn't easy," said Lesley, looking at Wilson and Frank, who each nodded to confirm his assessment. "We each selected the maximum number of exhibitors from the applications."

Frank nodded. "Even that was difficult given the high quality of pictured works."

"It was brutal," Wilson continued. "Then we met and the first thing we did was determine which artists had been selected by all three of us."

"Those were undisputed and were automatically accepted as exhibitors." Lesley looked down into the bottom of his empty glass. "Oddly, that represented about eighty percent of the 270 spaces. So, we felt pretty good about that much of it going so easily."

"But what we didn't know at that time"— Frank lowered his brows—"was how difficult choosing the remaining twenty percent was going to be."

"How true," Lesley continued. "The next category was for entrants who were selected by two of us. We asked the one who didn't choose the artist to defend his rejection, and if we agreed with his evaluation, we removed the artist from the list."

"But if we changed his mind, then that was a new exhibitor. We got up to ninety percent of the booths filled that way." Wilson signaled the bartender for fresh drinks.

Frank smiled. "But, honestly, the last twenty-five applications nearly killed us."

"Well, actually we nearly killed each other." Wilson noisily slurped on the ice of his drink.

Savannah mentally shook her head. *Every group*

has factions. The trick is to avoid being "captured" by one faction as well as to avoid seeming aloof. Politics are everywhere and my business now depends on how well I manage getting along with groups like this.

Frank chuckled. "It was a matter of getting a consensus among us for each artist by trying to convince the other two that the artist deserved admission."

"The real tragedy is that they all deserved admission," said Wilson, "but there was only booth space for another twenty-five."

Savannah quaffed the last of her champagne. "How did you choose?"

They all three looked at each other in turn and Frank shrugged his shoulders in a "who cares" gesture.

"You can't tell anyone." Frank lowered his voice and said, "We drew lots."

"You did what?" Savannah nearly dropped her champagne.

"Shush. Now you listen a second," Frank said as he held his hand out in a stop position. "The quality of the entrants was so very high, and we couldn't get even two of us to agree on the remaining choices. It worked out in the end."

Wilson continued, "Basically, we gave each of them a number, wrote the numbers on slips of paper, put them in a jar, then drew numbers in turn until we reached 270 exhibitors."

"It was really that simple," Lesley said. "Luck is one of the most important factors in succeeding in the fine arts."

Savannah laughed out loud and then shook

her head. "I certainly have to hand it to you for finding a creative solution when you became deadlocked."

Wilson added, "One of the necessary elements of a successful career in art is a generous and timely amount of pure luck. You're right: luck is vital."

"Just one question." She fingered her empty glass. "For my peace of mind, anyway. What group was Megan Loyola in?"

"Oh, she was one of the exhibitors in the first group," Frank said. "We all loved her work. The pieces in her booth were beyond exceptional—genius even. Her death is an enormous loss to the advancement of modern glassworks." The other two nodded solemnly. "Good call in selecting her for your top award."

"But her application was practically blank. There was only a picture of her central figure."

"Indeed," said Lesley. "It was unforgettable, wasn't it?"

Savannah tilted her head. "Yes, it was. One more question, and I promise this is my last. What group was Leon Price in?"

All three looked at one another and eye-signaled Frank to answer. "He is one lucky artist."

Savannah scrunched her brow. "What do you mean?"

Frank glanced at the others to see if they would say anything, then replied, "He's a little erratic. Some of his work is spectacular and then some of it is terrible. We didn't really know what kind of work he would display. As it turns out, he is in a spectacular phase. His number was the last one we drew as an accepted applicant."

"Oh, wow. He was incredibly lucky. You know he was my second choice for the best glass exhibit."

"Well, that's going to make him financially happier than he was before."

"Why? What do you mean?" Savannah knotted her brow. "He got five hundred for second place in glass."

Frank leaned closer to Savannah and lowered his voice. "There are whisperings of a reallocation of the prize monies since Megan didn't claim her award."

Savannah leaned back. "What! Why would they do that? Megan won the prize! It should go to her family or estate or something."

"Well, it appears that there's some small print in the application form that states if a prize winner does not claim the award—for any reason—the next highest scoring exhibitor is given the award."

Savannah narrowed her eyes. "That would certainly keep the money where it could be useful, but who wins the Best of Show prize money? That's a lot of money you're talking about."

"The leadership committee has determined the new winners, but they're not revealing it to anyone here."

"Why, for heaven's sake?"

"They want to wait a few days until the flurry of bad publicity on Megan's death has blown over—

maybe even until after the killer is identified—
and then hold a press conference to announce
the new winner."

"How do you know this?"

"Shhhh, let's get some privacy." Frank turned
to Lesley and Wilson. "Sorry, guys. We need to
talk a little glass business. See you later."

"Oh, thanks, you're taking away the prettiest
judge in the room!" Wilson protested.

"Not for long."

Frank took Savannah by the elbow.

"Hey." She pulled out of his grasp.

"Sorry, sorry." He nodded over to the opposite
corner of the room. His head swiveled around
like an owl trying to make sure no one would
overhear them.

"I know Wanda Quitman pretty well. She's an
absolutely fantastic organizer and publicist. Unfortunately, she doesn't know how to rein in
her opinions of how things should be run. I
knew about the change in plans less than an
hour after the prize committee had decided
what to do."

"So much for secrecy. So, Leon was already
the top winner in the glass category, but who
will get the grand prize?"

"That's where Leon's luck has turned viral,"
said Frank. "He is the committee's next choice."

"This will knock his socks off," Savannah said.
"He stormed off when he received first prize in
the glass category. It appears he was down to his

last fifty dollars and was going to have to give up his art."

"You mean that he—" Frank shuffled back a step.

"Yes, Frank, he got the highest rating behind Megan." *Another strike against Leon. Since he really needs the money, that would be a powerful motive—and he has no alibi.*

"So the overall second-place prize goes to the Moon Under Water bartender." Savannah was happy that Sam would get a prize. That small encouragement would make a big difference.

"You were spoiled for choice in the glass category. I hate to admit this, but even I couldn't have done better in selecting the winners. Although one of these years I'd like to try my hand as a judge."

Not while I have anything to say about it.

"Frank, one of the things I heard from another artist is that you and Megan had a big public argument on Saturday. What was that about?"

"No, that wasn't an argument. We were having a business discussion."

"That's not how I heard it. It appeared to get very heated and loud. That would be something the police would need to know."

He huffed up his chest. "I'm not in the business of doing police work. You're not still in touch with that detective, are you?"

"Sure, why not?"

"Wait a minute. Why is he in touch with you?"

"It's merely a matter of time and place," Savannah lied. "I found Megan's body. Remember?"

"Oh yeah, I heard that." He signaled to a waiter with a tray of drinks. He placed his tumbler on the tray and grabbed another scotch. Savannah placed her empty glass on the tray and waved the waiter away.

"What's wrong with you? Have another. It's free!"

"You know very well that I prefer beer, specifically craft beer. Anyway, I'm trying to be a good business owner and keep my head. I love champagne, but it gives me a buzz faster than anything else. I am a bit hungry, though."

She waved to one of the waiters carrying canapés and put several on one of the napkins stacked on his tray.

I'm getting nowhere. Now, what was I trying to find out from these high-society whizbangs?

"If you're not going to tell me about the argument, you can at least help me find out more about Megan. Her application has very little information on it. Did you guys read the background information on the applicants?"

"Nope, we weren't looking at anything but the pictures of the artworks. Her single photo was absolutely fantastic. Nothing else matters. Why do you want to know?"

"I'm merely curious. No reason."

"Are you going to continue working with the Spinnaker Art Festival?"

"Of course I am. If they'll have me. As the new owner of Webb's Glass Shop, it's about time I get more involved with community events. Dad was a longtime dedicated supporter."

Frank grumbled into his glass of scotch. "I'm sure they'll have you. You're the new darling of this year's Spinnaker Art Festival."

"Not true, Frank." She looked back into the room and spotted Keith entering the room. "Oh goodness, please excuse me, I've got to catch up with my former instructor, Keith, but I'm still curious about your argument with Megan. Just saying it looks suspicious. You might want to talk to Detective Parker about it—even better if you do it before I talk to him next."

She walked away from a very pale Frank, who took another scotch from the passing waiter's tray.

"Keith." She tapped him on the shoulder. "It's nice to see you here. How did you wrangle an invitation to this?"

He smiled wide. "Oh, it's my connection to the Pilchuck Glass School that gets me into these things."

"Of course, duh!" She lightly tapped a palm to her forehead. "How are you doing? I know you were close to Megan."

"When you work in a hot glass shop together, you reveal almost everything in the art. Megan, however, was a bit of a mystery. I mean, we were student and mentor, but she didn't get close to anyone that she didn't bed."

"Do you have any idea if she has family or anything about her background?"

"Odd, isn't it?" His voice softened. "I was her mentor for the past few months and basically she seemed to spring forth fully formed from the forehead of Zeus."

"There was literally no information on her application form. Doesn't that seem strange?"

"Well, the art world is not particularly interested in anyone's background. The art speaks for the artist, and Megan's art has a lot to say. The originality and quality of her work acted as a blank-check admittance to any place she wanted to either sell or exhibit." He shook his head slowly. "Such a loss."

"I found some shards from her display in the area behind her booth. It looks like they came from the central display piece. If I showed them to you, do you think you could identify the glass shop that she used to create it?"

He nodded. "Most likely. There are subtle differences among the major hot shops in the recipe that they use for their hot glass material."

"Would you need a microscope?"

"Not really. A good magnifying lamp with a light table would do quite well."

"I've got both at Webb's. Could you stop by tomorrow and see if you can identify the origin of her central masterpiece?"

"I'd be happy to, although it makes my gut twist to think of that piece being destroyed. Why on earth do you want to know?"

"Actually, I'm helping with the investigation.

It's especially important to me since at this point I'm the principal person of interest." She made air quotation marks with her fingers.

"That's crazy." He shook his head. "Who would think that?"

"I don't think Detective Parker is seriously convinced that I would have murdered Megan, but the fact remains that I was seen with her late on Saturday. Then, even worse, I was the one who found her. That's two trips to the top of the suspect list."

"What are you going to do?"

"I'm certainly not going to sit on my hands and wait for the police to investigate their way to the wrong suspect, namely, me. So, I've started my own investigation. Can you help?"

He folded Savannah into a side hug. "Of course, you don't have to ask."

Leaning into the hug, Savannah remembered how special she'd felt as his student. *This is how a good teacher influences their students.*

"Listen, now that I've said these things out loud, I'm getting concerned. Would you mind taking a look at the shards tonight?"

Keith squeezed her a little tighter and looked into her eyes. "Of course, it would be my pleasure. Let's get out of this social honey trap and get into some glass."

"I've got to stop by the house to get the shards and let my dog out. I'll meet you at Webb's in about an hour." She looked down at her watch. "That would be at about ten o'clock. Good?"

"More than good." He smiled.

Chapter 12

The shop was dark except for the light in the display and retail room that burned continuously as a cursory deterrent to break-ins. Savannah unlocked the custom workshop door and turned on the large eight-by-ten-foot light box. She had a work in progress lying on top, but it didn't cover the entire surface. She rearranged the work to one side so that there was a clear area at the foot of the table.

Next, she went to her dad's worktable and grabbed his large magnifying glass and also the set of magnifiers that you wear over your head like a baseball cap. As soon as she placed them on the light table, she heard a series of taps at the front door.

"Perfect timing," she said as she unlocked the door for Keith and pulled it wide. "I've got everything set up."

Keith stepped into the display and retail room.

"Wow, you've got a fantastic shop. How long has it been here?"

"It's been in the family since the twenties, when Grandfather Roy started designing and restoring pieces for the local churches. It was already well established when my dad took it over in nineteen fifty-seven. I've been running it for only a couple of months, and, believe me, I didn't give my dad enough credit for how effortlessly he appeared to keep everything going."

Savannah walked him into the custom workshop. He walked over to the light box worktable and stared down at the work in progress. "Is this typical?"

"Yes, it's a restoration project. My client found the panel in a large wooden box at an auction in Tampa. It was part of a lot of three matched works. The smaller panels were still intact and only needed a little cleanup and repair. This one was severely damaged, and a lot of the individual pieces are incredibly dirty and broken."

Keith walked down to the other end of the worktable. "How are you cleaning it up?"

"Carefully." Savannah adjusted a few of the newly cleaned parts. "Amanda is my main volunteer and we first started by washing the glass. That didn't make a dent because this window was obviously installed on the bad weather side of a building."

"Of course"—he picked up one of the pieces—"but it looks like this might have been victim to a roof runoff as well. This is encrusted with layers of dirt."

"I tried soaking the pieces in a strong cleaner in longer and longer periods of time all the way up to twenty-four hours. That made the cleaning process a little better, but we were still spending hours and hours scrubbing, rinsing, and cleaning."

"Tedious."

"Very, so we started using a cloth buffing wheel on a tiny handheld drill."

"What on earth made you think of that?"

"One of our long-term students saw us struggling and suggested that we try the cloth buffer method. He does a lot of woodworking as well and uses the buffer drill for final polishing of the wooden pens that he makes. It's cut the work down by ninety percent, and we'll be done with the cleaning in about three weeks, instead of three months. My clients are fabulous about waiting as long as it takes to restore a panel to perfection."

Savannah reached into her backpack and pulled out the baggie that she had used for collecting the shards. "Here are the shards that Edward and I found behind the area where Megan's exhibit booth was installed," she said as she spilled them onto the surface of the light table.

Keith drew up a work stool and bent over the shards. "These are pretty small." He picked up the magnifying glass and examined them as they lay on the light table.

"Do you have a pair of tweezers?"

"Sure." She got a pair from her workbench and placed them in his right hand.

He grunted. Then he picked up the largest shard with the tweezers and held it closer to the lens. He placed it back on the light table and pulled the eyeglass magnifiers over his head and adjusted the fit using the screw in the back.

Leaning over to examine the tiny slivers, he said, "Hmm, interesting."

"What's interesting?" Savannah leaned over, too.

He picked up the magnifying glass again. "Very interesting."

"Stop with the Sherlock Holmes shtick. What's interesting?"

He straightened up and his face turned a pale shade of yellow. "This is not good at all."

"Tell me."

"Here, let me show you what's bothering me. Put on the magnifying glasses."

Savannah pulled the magnifiers over her head and adjusted them tight around her head. She leaned over the light table. "I see the shards, but what am I looking for?"

"Do you see the red running through the clear glass?"

"No, just red glass."

Keith handed her the magnifying glass. "Now, can you see?"

Savannah looked through the double magnifiers and exhaled a long, low whistle. "This is a type of glass that I have never seen before." She stood up straight and removed the glasses.

"Where did this come from? Not the Seattle studio."

"Nope, we don't have this kind of glass. That doesn't mean that it isn't a new process that I haven't seen." Keith crossed his arms and began to pace the small workroom.

"This is why her pieces are so vibrant," Savannah said. "She was using a process that intensified the red throughout the molten glass. It looks like she didn't start with clear glass, like in every other hot shop I've ever been to."

"So where did she create the pieces in the exhibit?"

Savannah sat on the stool that Keith had abandoned. "I was told that she and her team had been using McCloud's hot shop after hours."

"So, no one was around when she created these pieces."

"Apparently not."

They fell silent for a moment, and then Keith sighed. "I'm stumped. I can't figure out how she made this glass. Red is really tricky to work with and a consistent process would be worth a fortune to the big glass manufacturers." He stopped pacing. "This could be the motive you're looking for. This could be what is worth killing Megan."

"Her team would know. Her pieces would demand a team of two or three to execute." Savannah placed the magnifying glass back on her dad's workbench.

"We'll have to ask her studio partner. He's one of the interns that I sent from Seattle."

"Which one, Leon or Vincent?"

"Leon Price, the one who had a booth across from Megan's."

"Yes, I loved his booth—his work was really powerful. How well do you know him?" Savannah pulled up another work stool and rested one foot on the bottom rung.

"Not that well. He has a wild temper and works on his art by himself."

"That doesn't sound like a good candidate for teamwork."

"It's complicated. His temper is usually directed at his own failures or mistakes. When he's part of a team, he becomes invisible. The best type of work partner when making a hot glass project is the one who basically becomes an extension of you during the creation process. He could do that, so he was in high demand and could afford to be selective with who he worked with."

"Why did he want to come to St. Petersburg?"

"I don't know." Keith rubbed the back of his neck. "Motivation for artists is not a reliable tool for selecting intern candidates. Most are looking for inspiration or a change in scenery. Either is usually effective to start a new thread of productivity."

Savannah remembered what Keith had said about Megan only opening up to those she took to bed. If she and Leon had been close, maybe he had more information on her.

"When did they part?"

"I think they were lovers quite recently, but

since Leon is cranky, I figured Megan had moved on."

"Do you know her current boyfriend—if she had one?"

Keith shook his head. "It could be anybody in her circle. She was a serial destroyer of hearts. It had been the cause of quite a few team shuffles." He sighed deeply, then looked down. "It was the driving inspiration behind her works. She called it the flame of new love and the ashes of broken love."

"I wish I could have known her." Savannah turned off the light table. "She sounds like one of those amazing bigger-than-life personalities."

"A pretty dangerous way to find a muse, if you ask me."

"Who might know about her current love?" Savannah asked.

"No clue. It could be anyone."

"Do you know where she was staying? Maybe her neighbors will know more about her personal life."

"Good idea." He patted his pockets and delved into the right-hand one. "Here's her address. I wrote it on the back of my card. She wanted me to stop by tomorrow before I headed back to Seattle."

"Thanks, I'll add that to our list. I know you talked to Leon, but what about Vincent?" Savannah asked.

"I haven't been able to find him anywhere. I've called his cell, but he's not answering, which is very unusual. My students are typically very responsive to my calls."

"What about her family?"

"Just like everything else I've known about Megan, her family life was complicated and volatile."

"How?" Savannah took a small envelope from the bottom drawer of one of the workbenches.

"Megan was from Seattle and had an older sister who was the darling of her parents. You know the story—honor student, valedictorian, full scholarship to Harvard Law School, and now she's a famous legal thriller author with a television show that she produces. Megan was the unruly, wild-child dropout with emotional issues."

"Are her parents still living?" Savannah used a pair of tweezers to pick up the glass shards and put them in the small envelope.

"Yes, but from what I gather, they hadn't spoken in years. Her sister had recently married the director of her television series and then followed that up with a baby boy. The first grandchild and a boy to boot. Tough act to follow."

"But Megan was beginning to enjoy some success. Her recent streak of Best of Show wins and prize money awards must have impressed." Savannah tucked in the flap to the envelope and placed it on the light table.

"I'm not sure, but I got the feeling that Megan thought she was about to be validated for choosing to be a glass artist."

"She was well on her way to becoming an important emerging artist. She would have been the newest young thing at the galleries next year. She could have made it. That's what is so sad. All that talent and drive gone."

"I'm not looking forward to talking to her parents." Keith lowered his eyes and shook his head slowly. "They're arriving late tonight. I'm going to help them with making funeral arrangements."

"Oh, then you're not leaving tomorrow?"

"No, I'm staying until this is resolved. I can't leave with a former student dead. I'm ready to help you in any way I can."

"I would be grateful if you could join my investigation team. You can be a huge help at the Duncan McCloud Gallery. Amanda's already been there, but she's merely a student. Since you're a visiting professor from the famous Pilchuck Glass School, they would be delighted to have you tour their facilities."

"That shouldn't make a difference. This is murder we're talking about."

"Right, but I'm not the police. You actually know her family. I think that is going to be an important point. If you don't mind, we'll go over together after class tomorrow. Is that good?"

"It's good for me. I was originally scheduled to fly back to Seattle tomorrow afternoon, but I canceled my return ticket, so my schedule is open. Sadly, not the best way to get some extra time in St. Petersburg."

Chapter 13

Savannah arrived at Webb's early and was surprised to find Jacob deeply involved in sorting the Spinnaker Art Festival artist applications into yet another configuration of stacks. His service beagle, Suzy, followed each step that Jacob took along the length of the worktable looking up to read his face. Suzy's rubber booties padded softly on the tile floor in her quest to stay close beside him. She was alert and ready to warn him or Savannah if an anxiety attack was imminent and he would need the medication that was stored in her service vest.

"Any luck?"

Jacob looked up at Savannah and gave a noncommittal shrug of his thin shoulders. "I have sorted them by various parameters. Once alphabetically, then chronologically by date received, and now I'm organizing them by location." He returned his full focus to his concentrated task.

"But did you find anything?"

Jacob looked up as if he couldn't believe she had asked the question. "Not yet. I would have said." He returned to the task with the same intensity that he had applied to the first sorting of the papers.

I'd better call his mother to make sure she knows he's doing this. I know he promised to tell her, but a teenager doesn't always share everything with their parents. He's definitely good at this and he's certainly enjoying it.

She looked at the envelope containing the red shards on the light table and spilled them out onto the surface. Images returned of Megan's haunting exhibit and the firestorms that had been created in the wake of her adventurous life. Savannah carefully placed the shards back in the envelope and went to the back of her shop to put them in her backpack.

Jacob's mother worked as a judge in the juvenile court over in Tampa. Dialing Frances Underwood's cell, she expected that it would roll over to voice mail.

"Hi, Savannah. Are you calling about the booties? Are they working out or is there something wrong? They were the devil to find. We had to get her used to wearing them a little bit longer every day but Jacob was definitely motivated."

"The booties are terrific and it makes her so

happy to be with Jacob instead of isolated from him by staying in my office. I wish my students were so enthusiastic about our rule for wearing standard closed-toe shoes."

"Okay," Frances paused, "is everything good with Jacob?"

"Jacob's doing fine. He's growing into a skilled, dependable apprentice. I wanted to talk with you about his latest investigation project."

"Investigation? Not like the last time."

"No, no, Frances. Nothing like that."

"It was such a strain."

"I do understand. Officially, I'm a suspect in the Spinnaker Art Festival murder, but in reality Detective Parker isn't taking that seriously. I feel a strong connection to Megan: she was my age, studying at my studio, shared my instructors. I plan to do everything I can to solve this case."

There was complete silence on the line.

Savannah held her breath.

Frances chuckled loudly. "So this is different how?"

Savannah could hear the irony. "You're right. I've gotten myself into another mess."

"Okay, okay. How can I help?"

"Has Jacob talked to you about this?"

There was a long silence. "Obviously, no." Frances's voice was low and crisp.

"I was afraid of that." Savannah had guessed right that Jacob had failed to get permission to analyze the artist applications.

"I need to take advantage of Jacob's skills in pattern matching and data analysis."

"I'm sorry, he hasn't said anything about it."

"I should have called you earlier. I keep forgetting that he's a teenager because he acts so mature here in the shop." Savannah toyed with the idea of having him stop, but actually she was in a tight spot and needed his help. "He was supposed to tell you about analyzing some data for me. I'm investigating the death of a glass artist at the Spinnaker Art Festival."

"So you need his pattern-matching skills?"

"Yes, he leapt right into an analysis of a huge database. I thought he could spot something within a few hours, but this is taking more time than I expected, so I thought I'd better check with you so that you know what he's doing to help me."

"You have our full support, Savannah. If you hadn't solved your dad's murder so quickly, we might still be mired in the myriad channels of the justice system. It was made worse by the logical and believable fact that Jacob appeared to be the only credible candidate for murdering not only your dad, but his associate as well. We will be grateful to you for as long as we live."

"I was lucky to have made a difference."

"Whatever you need Jacob to do is fine by me. My one request is that you keep me up to date with what's happening. If you can think of any way that I can help, simply let me know."

"Thanks a lot, Frances. It's a deal," Savannah said and quickly ended the call.

The front-door bell jangled on its hook. "Hey, luv. How are you this morning?" Edward carried a tray of coffee and croissants into the small office at the back and placed it on the pull-out shelf of the rolltop desk. "You look a bit blue. Are you okay?"

"Nope"—she reached for one of the warm croissants—"but this will help enormously."

"Good." He poured a steaming cup of coffee and handed it over. "Um, I have some news from over the pond."

"From what?"

Edward sighed deeply. "From England. You know, where I'm from—England."

"I know that." She took an enormous bite of the fresh croissant. "This is heaven."

Edward shifted from foot to foot. "It's like this—my parents are coming over for their spring visit. They visit over here for several weeks in the spring, then again in the summer, and also over the Christmas holiday. So it doesn't really mean anything, anything at all that they are coming over."

Savannah choked on her croissant and Edward patted her on the back.

"Are you all right? Do you need a drink? Anyway, I'm having some concerns."

"About . . ."

"About meeting my parents. They're very old-fashioned."

"You have no—" Savannah stood straight up, slopping the coffee down her leg. "Ouch! Ouch! Ouch!" She grabbed one of the cloth napkins on the tray and dabbed the worst of the liquid from her jeans.

Where did that come from? Why am I upset? His folks are probably adorable.

She pinched a bit of the denim in her fingers and held it away from her skin.

"I'm sorry, that was clumsy. In any case, we still haven't found a credible suspect and it's already Wednesday."

"Don't get nervous. I think we need more help."

Savannah flopped back into her office chair, which shrieked a squeak that threatened to split the seat. "I've got more help."

"Who?"

"Keith has offered to help."

"Oh." Edward began gathering up the cups and napkins.

"Don't 'Oh' me. I've known him for a long time. He'll be able to research into Megan's background much easier than any of us can. He says he knows her family."

Edward took a deep breath. "Yes, I get that." He finished loading up the tray. "But I don't have to like it."

Why is he upset? Why am I upset?

The unlocking of the back door broke her thoughts.

"Good morning." Amanda bustled through

the door, hampered by a gigantic designer bag hanging across her body and multiple plastic grocery bags straining deep ribbons into her plump arms. "I'm a little early," she panted, "but I wanted to bring in some samples of finished pieces for the class."

Savannah looked at her with her head tilted. "We have samples already in the display and retail room."

"Yes, but Dale wanted to see mine." She grinned from ear to ear. "He asked especially to see my finished pieces."

Savannah pressed her lips into a bemused smile. "That's very sweet. He's a nice boy."

"I'll put these in the custom workshop for Dale to see."

"Sorry, that won't work. Jacob has every available surface taken up with his analysis of the Spinnaker Art Festival artist applications."

"Oh." Amanda's face fell in on itself.

"Why don't you arrange them on the light table in the display and retail room? They'll look fantastic there."

Her eyes lit up. "Yes! That's a great idea." She made her way into the display and retail room and Savannah could hear the glass clinks announcing the unloading and arranging of Amanda's collection of fused dishes on the light table.

Smiling, Savannah looked at their whiteboard and picked up the dry-erase pen and wrote "Relatives" under the Suspect column. Then she added "Research Megan's family" to the Investigation column and assigned Keith to the task.

"When I look at this, I realize some of them are leads, not suspects. I need another column." She started to draw a vertical line on the whiteboard.

"No, no. Don't get complicated." Edward took the marker out of her hand and added a "/Leads" to the Suspect column title. "Simple. Simple is good." He then added an "S" or an "L" to each element in the column.

They looked at the updated whiteboard:

The Case of Megan Loyola's Murder

Suspect/Leads	Investigation	Assigned To
Frank Lattimer (S)	Subject of argument at festival	Savannah
Vincent O'Neil (S)	Megan's team member	Savannah
Wanda Quitman (S)	Upset Megan at reception	Edward
Glass shards (L)	Identify origin	Savannah
Registration forms (L)	Find connection patterns in application database	Jacob
Leon Price (S)	Megan's ex-boyfriends	Savannah
Relatives (L)	Research Megan's family	Keith

Savannah smiled. "I think this is enough to report to Detective Parker. I'll call for an appointment this afternoon." She smiled even bigger. "This might be enough to convince him to take me off the suspect list."

Edward frowned. "You still don't have an alibi."

"Details, details."

Chapter 14

Wednesday Morning

Savannah looked at her watch for the tenth time in as many minutes.

Will this class ever end? Crap, some teacher I am.

"That looks terrible." Rachel pointed to the small tower of glass that Faith had stacked on a piece of white kiln paper. "It's going to turn out to be a pile of mud."

"You don't know that." Faith circled her arms over the pile of pink, white, red, and clear glass that Rachel was threatening to tumble. "Savannah, tell Rachel to stop pestering me. She thinks my puddle will turn into a pile of mud."

Savannah walked back to the last row of student desks to yet again mediate an argument between the twins. Standing by Faith's stack of silver dollar–sized glass pieces, she said, "I think this is going to fuse into a beautiful puddle of glass."

Faith stuck her tongue out at Rachel. "I told you I was doing it right."

"Class, this is a good example of what I was demonstrating earlier this morning."

She pointed to Faith's work surface. "Faith has used several of the suggestions that I explained. The glass pieces are small but not uniform in size. The colors are compatible and complementary. Lastly, she has included a generous amount of clear glass to give the fused puddle texture and a see-through quality that will be interesting."

Up shot Miss Carter's hand. "Miss Webb, I'm confused. How is this stack of glass going to puddle? I don't get it."

"Okay, let me try explaining it another way." Savannah walked back to the front of the classroom. "Essentially, we're manufacturing our own sheet of glass so we can use it in creating new bowls, platters, or anything that uses fused glass as a component."

Dale spoke up, "How do you like to use it?"

Amanda piped in, "She uses it for her jewelry. Show them."

Savannah removed her right earring. "Here, you can see on the back the stripes formed by the four colors that I used. But on the front"— she turned the earring—"it's a swirl of the colors plus clear. That's interesting and unique." She passed the earring around the class.

Janice squinted. "But this stack won't be the right size for an earring."

"You are absolutely right, it won't. Tomorrow we'll look at our puddles and figure out what we want to do with them. More often than not, it can take up to three kiln firings to get the shape and size I want for jewelry, but only one or two firings when using molds."

"Are we going to have time?" asked Gary.

"Yes, there's time for two firings before class ends. If more firings are needed to complete your piece, you can come into the shop next week and pick them up. That's why it's not a mainstream production technique. It takes quite a bit of planning and multiple firings to get the effect."

At the ringing of the front-door bell, she nodded over to Amanda, signaling her to take care of whoever had arrived.

Savannah lifted her chin and smiled. *That's how a good teacher works.*

"It's nearly time to quit for the day, so leave your glass stack on your workbench and we'll get them in the kiln tonight."

"Just a second." Gary took out his cell phone and took a picture of his stack of red, white, and clear glass. "I'm going to post this to my Facebook page."

"Good idea," said Savannah. "That's something I need to start working on pretty soon—a social media presence is expected these days."

Amanda poked her head around the classroom

door. "Savannah, it's Keith. He said you were both going over to the Duncan McCloud Gallery?"

"Right, tell him I'll be ready to go in a few minutes."

Savannah walked around among the student worktables and suggested a few adjustments to the students' stacks. She walked the students out the door, then waited until they had all gone before she turned to Keith. "Whew! How do you manage to be so calm when you teach? I'm still a mess of nerves and get flustered, tongue-tied, and always manage to drop something—not good when you're teaching fused glass."

Keith chuckled. "Who says I'm calm? You only have to look calm and unworried. If you look calm, students think you are calm. Only the best teachers worry about how they are instructing. The bad teachers don't. Try not to worry; you're a good teacher."

"Thanks, I appreciate that." She turned to go back to the classroom. "All I have to do is load up the kiln and then we'll go over to McCloud's."

Amanda shook her head. "Don't be silly. You get yourself on your way. I can load up the kiln and then you can check my work when you get back. Then I want you to teach me how to program the digital beast. Good?"

"That's a great idea. Thanks bunches." Savannah gave her a quick hug and rushed into the office to grab her backpack, then looked at Keith and said, "Let's go do our sleuthing. Are you sure you want to do this?"

"Sure, this will be a hoot. Why not?"

"There is the distinct likelihood that we may be reported to the police. There is also a chance of some danger. We are trying to find a killer, you know—this is not to be taken lightly."

His eyes narrowed slightly. "Right."

It was a very quick drive to the Duncan McCloud Gallery. Keith parked his rental car in front of the studio. "It doesn't look very busy." He looked around the nearly empty parking lot.

"It hasn't been open very long. I think only about eight months. I hear it gets busy on the weekends, especially when there's a Friday Night Art Walk. Sometimes he has a gallery opening, which is usually accompanied by an artist lecture at the Museum of Fine Arts downtown. The combination attracts crowds for both venues. He's a good promoter."

The building was obviously a repurposed warehouse that had been painted an upscale burnt umber and had a new entrance that opened directly into the gallery. Keith and Savannah stood inside the threshold in silence. The exhibits were museum quality and displayed with a professional perfection of staging and mood. There were exhibit areas on each side of the building with another aisle down the middle. Each artist had a placard with a photograph of the artist along with a biographical sketch.

"Wow, this is New York City fancy," Savannah whispered. "My little shop looks like a kindergarten playroom compared to this. Are we still in St. Petersburg? I feel a little like Dorothy in Oz."

He looked around at the displayed pieces. "The variety of work is tremendous." He took Savannah by the elbow and pointed up to the tall ceiling. "Look at—"

"Welcome to the Duncan McCloud Gallery." Keith was interrupted as an athletic man with salt–and–pepper hair in a well-used industrial apron over pressed chino trousers and tailored white shirt walked gracefully from an office on the right side of the gallery. "I'm Duncan, the managing director. How can I help you?"

"Hi, I'm Keith Irving from the Pilchuck Glass School." He leaned forward to shake hands.

"I'm Savannah Webb, owner of Webb's Glass Shop in the Grand Central District up the street." Savannah noted the strong handshake, which she returned in kind.

"Oh, you're John Webb's daughter, right?"

Pleased that he knew her, Savannah replied, "Yes, I've taken over Webb's and I've been meaning to come down and see your place. The artworks are stunning and the display room is beyond fantastic."

"Thanks, it's a privilege to work with so many talented artists. St. Petersburg is on the cusp of becoming a world-class art destination."

Keith folded his arms. "It seems that the installation of the new Dali Museum not only attracted the Chihuly Museum permanent exhibit, but has encouraged other international artists to find workspaces in the city."

"It's true. That and the beautiful waterfront condos and gorgeous weather have attracted enthusiastic art patrons to the area. Very important," said Duncan."

Savannah tilted her head back. "So you're the owner?"

"Oh, I'm a minority partner. My wife is the majority partner for business reasons—she's extraordinarily talented with the paperwork, taxes, accounting, and most of the promotion responsibilities. I oversee the fun part—making art and teaching students." A playful grin made a quick appearance. "Anyway, since this is your first visit, let me show you around."

Savannah waved her hand at the large gallery. "This is a huge space. How many artists are exhibiting here?"

Duncan led them down the left-hand aisle. "At last count, it was over fifty. We have a mix of traveling artists and the work that my senior students produce. Would you like to see the studio?"

"Yes, yes," said Savannah. "It's been a few months since I've stepped into a working hot glass studio. I miss it."

Opening a set of industrial double doors, he said, "Let me know how this compares to Pilchuck's workspace. I keep meaning to visit there. I've only studied the layout through pictures."

The hot shop area was a tall, open-sided shed

with two walls missing to allow massive venting and permit visitors to watch from a portable aluminum grandstand located on the right-hand side of the massive furnaces.

"The team at the far left are intermediate students. They're planning a large vessel and are laying out the glass pick-ups they're going to need on the table. The team in the center are also intermediate students who have picked up their first glass gather out of the furnace. On the right are beginning students. They're creating small vases using only the most basic glass-blowing techniques. After one student makes a piece, they switch roles and the other one makes the same piece."

"How many students in a class?"

"I keep the classes small, limited to six. It works out nicely with the three furnaces. I find I can produce better students at a higher rate by keeping the numbers down. I can handle three classes a day."

"That's very similar to the approach my dad used." Savannah shifted her focus from Duncan to trying to watch the three teams. The team using the furnace nearest her had completed their vase and were preparing to detach it from the blowing tube. "Why are you mixing beginners with intermediate students?"

"It's one of my operational rules to have only one pair of beginning students in the hot shop at a time—working on the left only. They're still learning the protocols and safety issues involved in glass blowing. It keeps the work area safer and definitely calmer."

"Speaking of students"—Savannah smiled—"Keith and I are trying to verify where Megan Loyola created her flame torso works. Was it here?"

McCloud stood a bit taller. "Of course. I have the only studio capable of such large works. She was here all last week working her team into exhaustion to get her centerpiece for the Spinnaker Art Festival."

Keith nodded. "We thought it had to be here. What about her assistants?"

"Nope, didn't meet them. I looked in at one point. Megan was incredibly skilled and had two fellows helping her, but I didn't want to interrupt them." He paused and watched his students. "This is the hold-your-breath moment," Duncan spoke quietly. "A piece isn't done until it's safely detached from the blowing tube and resting in the cooling kilns."

The seated student of the pair deftly cracked off the vase into the second student's waiting pair of heavy gloves and then the second student carefully cradled the little vase while waiting for the other student to open the kiln doors. "Hey! This kiln is cold and there's already a piece in here."

"Go to the next kiln before it cracks!" the second student yelled.

The first student opened the next kiln, which was thankfully empty, and the second student placed the vase upright on the shelf inside and the first student closed the doors.

"Mr. McCloud, someone's left a large work in one of the curing kilns," said the first student.

"That's not permitted." He automatically grabbed a heavy pair of gloves and pulled them on while he strode over to the first curing kiln and pulled open the doors. "I don't understand. This shouldn't be here."

Savannah looked into the kiln. "No, it shouldn't be here, but I'm glad it's turned up."

"What is it?" Keith looked over their shoulders.

Swallowing the lump in her throat she replied, "That's Megan's Best of Show piece from the Spinnaker Art Festival. You'd better call the police—it's evidence."

Chapter 15

Savannah wasted precious minutes trying to find a parking space along the crowded Central Avenue. The main drag in St. Petersburg wasn't named Main Street like in most small towns in the South. Perhaps because a Russian founded it and named it after his beloved hometown.

Focus, Savannah, don't get lost in trivia.

She drove slowly past all the full spots and even checked the parking lot of the midcentury antique store. It was full, with an attendant collecting fees for the Rays game. Disgusted, she turned around and searched again.

Please, please, please, somebody pull out!

She resorted to stalking pedestrians who might be heading toward their car and spotted one pulling out of a prime spot in front of Ferg's Grill. A lumbering double-cab full-bed truck was approaching the spot at the same time. She quickly whipped across traffic and drove her agile Mini into the space during the few seconds when there was enough room to slip into the spot. The driver of the monster truck was not happy and rolled down the window shouting, "Hey! That spot was mine."

She agreed with him completely, but shrugged her shoulders and smiled an apology. She waited until he had moved on before climbing out, then locking the Mini.

Dammit! I'm late. Late. Late. Late.

Stepping through the main entrance to the St. Petersburg Police Department at five minutes past three, she could feel her heart beating a staccato.

Calm down. Relax.

She inhaled deeply and mentally practiced the opening moves of her Tai Chi meditation practice. It was her surefire fix. Her heart rate dropped almost immediately.

You haven't done anything wrong. You're helping, remember. You're helping as well as clearing yourself.

The reception desk was staffed with a smiling, slick-haired hipster version of Mayberry's Deputy Fife from *The Andy Griffith Show.* He was gawky, cadaver skinny, and had a habit of repeatedly pushing his oversized black glasses back up his nose. Savannah walked up to the desk. "I have an appointment with Detective Parker, please."

"Yes, ma'am. May I see your identification, ma'am?"

A quick dip down into her backpack produced her billfold. Savannah pulled out her driver's license and the Barney look-alike examined it with meticulous care. "I'll notify Detective Parker that you're here." He handed her a plastic visitor's badge attached to a metal clip. "Wear this at all times. Please proceed through the screening booth and wait in the reception room to the left. Detective Parker will send an escort."

Rats, I forgot about the screening. Do I have anything bad with me?

She placed her backpack on the short conveyor belt. She looked at the attendant's face as she quickly patted her pockets and pulled out a small pair of needle-nose pliers, a two-foot length of copper necklace chain, and a half dozen glass pendants.

"I make jewelry." She displayed her best "innocent as the day is long" smile.

The attendant didn't look even mildly surprised. He picked up the pliers, gave them a trial, put them back in the bin, and then waved her on through the scanning machine.

No beeps—yay!

She sat on an overengineered industrial chair that was so old it had become fashionable again. The leather and metal look, which had been popular in the late sixties, had worn well. In fact, the entire building had worn well and there was talk about the police station being added to the National Register of Historic Buildings. The sad truth was that although the original construction had been costly, there had never been budget for additions or remodeling. As a result, the building was frozen in a time warp and deserving of the designation. It was unique in the South.

Just as she was considering pulling out her pliers and working on the new necklace, the elevators opened and Officer Boulli looked around at the seats and then walked toward her.

He's gained even more weight.

Smiling broadly to hide her distaste, Savannah stood and held out her hand. "It's nice to see you again, Officer Boulli."

He wiped his right hand down the seam of his uniform trousers, then shook hands. "Hi there, Miss Webb, I'm glad you remember me."

"I'm hardly going to forget the case that caused me so much grief."

He pointed a chubby finger right at her nose. "You nearly got me fired."

"Me? How did I do that?"

Officer Boulli drew his finger back and rocked back and forth on his heels glaring down at Savannah. "I don't know 'xactly, but I think you had something to do with my suspension."

Of course I did, but I'm not going to admit it. Ever. Ever. Ever.

"Is Detective Parker ready to see me?"

"Yep. Follow me, Miss Webb." His words were clipped and crisp.

He turned and pressed the button to the elevator, then led her down to Detective Parker's office. "Here's Miss Webb, sir."

"Thanks, Officer Boulli." Detective Parker stood. "Don't leave. I'd like for you to stay and help me with Miss Webb's statement. Miss Webb, please have a seat."

Savannah thought the new office suited Detective Parker perfectly. There was precisely enough room for his desk, chair, and even a tiny round conference table. The two file cabinets meant that he could keep all the flat surfaces clear. He must be pleased because she knew him to be almost obsessed with order and calm in his workspace.

"It's Savannah, please call me Savannah. I feel as though we've shared too many once in a lifetime events to be so formal."

"I agree. Well, in that case, I'd be pleased to call you Savannah. We have indeed been through an uncommon number of unusual experiences. Please sit." He waved Officer Boulli to the remaining visitor's chair, then sat himself.

Officer Boulli sucked in his gut and sat tentatively to ensure that his shirt buttons took the strain. He looked enormously uncomfortable.

Savannah smiled.

Detective Parker pointed a finger directly at her chest. "You didn't tell me that you were present when they found Megan's masterpiece at the Duncan McCloud Gallery. Did you think they wouldn't mention that when we investigated?"

"I—" Savannah choked on her protest. She turned a bright red. After clearing her throat, she said, "I knew that they would call you and that I was going to meet with you this afternoon."

She lifted her chin. "I'm here now. What would you like to know?"

Parker rolled his eyes. "Savannah, you would try the patience of Job. Seriously, why do you think Megan's artwork was there?"

"Honestly? I think it was one of the safest places in the city to store it. Any one of the glass artists who found it would recognize it and take proper care of it. It's heavy and fragile, a risky combination."

"Who do you think put it there?"

"Someone who is familiar with McCloud's facilities."

Parker frowned. "Well that narrows it down to every glassworker in the city."

"That's right. And because the hot shop is open and booked around the clock, all of them have access to the studio. I don't think it's a helpful lead, but I'm very happy that her masterpiece wasn't destroyed. It's her legacy."

Detective Parker nodded his head slightly, then handed Savannah a manila folder. "This is a transcript of your statement from the scene on Monday morning. I would like for you to read it over again, make any changes you feel are necessary to describe your actions clearly, initial each change, and then finally I need your signature at the bottom." He handed her a pen.

"Before I forget"—she put the folder and pen on the edge of his desk then reached into her backpack and pulled out the envelope of glass shards—"Edward and I found these in the grass near Megan's festival booth."

Parker stood up. "What? You've been—"

"Snooping around? Yes, I have. They were hidden in a patch of grass to the rear of her booth. Edward found them by using his fingers. He has stitches. We had to get them out of the grass. A child or dog could have been seriously hurt. Anyway, I've examined them and they look like the shards that were embedded in her wound."

"Hand them over." He took them and sat back down. He handed the manila folder to her.

Savannah opened the folder, and began to read her statement. The printed sentences were facts expressed on the page in dry, emotionless words. Still, they summoned the shock of raw violence back into her mind with a rush of sorrow and dismay.

Her signature looked a little wonky, but Savannah handed the folder and the pen back to Detective Parker. "It's quite accurate." She was conscious of the warmth rising from her throat into her cheeks and dancing across her forehead. She used the palm of her hand to swipe her brow and summoned calm thoughts.

Puppies. Playfully romping puppies . . .

Rooney stopping short, pointing at the seawall.

Damn it, not that. Roses. Wonderfully fragrant roses bursting into bloom.

The raw, red wound on Megan's scalp.

"Are you okay?" Detective Parker stood. "Can I get you a glass of water?"

"That sounds good." She leaned back in the

chair and waved her hand in front of her face. "I'm feeling a little woozy."

"Quick! Put your head down. Yep, down. That's it." Parker opened a tiny fridge under the table behind his desk and pulled out a fresh bottle of spring water.

When she started to lift up again, Detective Parker stretched his hands out and said, "Nope, not yet. You still don't have much color."

"This is ridiculous," she muttered. She inhaled deeply and long several times. Then finally felt the darkness begin to recede.

"That's better." Parker had walked around the desk and pressed three fingers on her wrist feeling her pulse. "Okay, raise up slowly, very slowly and lean back in the chair." He twisted the water bottle open and handed it to Savannah. "Here, take a few swigs of this."

She took a long swig of the lovely cold water and then inhaled a deep, ragged breath.

Parker watched her carefully. "That was close. You have some color back. How do you feel?"

"Embarrassed." She gulped another swig of water. "I don't know what came over me."

"It's rare to have a strong reaction to the description of a violent event. It does happen, but not very often. I should have warned you. I apologize."

"Apparently, I've been concentrating on the actions of the living Megan and had pushed the violence of her death completely out of my mind. I'm sorry."

"What do you mean by concentrating on the actions of the living Megan?"

I shouldn't have said that.

Savannah squirmed in the chair. "Well, it seems to me that the only way for me to get off your suspect list would be to find out more about Megan from the perspective of a glass artist."

Detective Parker leaned forward, steepling his fingers in front of his mouth. He looked pointedly at Officer Boulli and then back to Savannah. "You know it's against the law to interfere in the investigation of a crime. I'm sure you know that because we've had this conversation before."

What does he mean by that? Is he angry?

"Typically, Savannah, someone clears their name from the suspect list by discrediting their means to the murder—by providing an alibi, for example."

Leaning forward a fraction, she stared at him. "I don't have an alibi. I was home with Rooney. That's not an alibi, but this is happening in my world. It's happening to me. It's happening in my complicated and confusing world of artists, galleries, festivals, and studios. I know these people. I know how they think and I know how they work. You need me."

As he leaned back in his chair, a small smile skittered quickly around the corners of his mouth and then vanished. He leaned forward again. "You are absolutely right. But because you are a suspect, I can't do that."

"But . . ."

Parker raised his hand for her to be quiet. "Hear me out. I don't know for a fact that you had anything to do with Megan's death. I have no concrete evidence."

"Well, that's a relief."

"But that does nothing for the law or for our internal investigation policies and procedures. So for now, I'm planning to hire Frank Lattimer as my expert consultant to give us insight into the behind-the-scenes rarified world of glass artists."

Savannah felt her teeth clench. "But he's such an idiot. You can't possibly take what he says seriously."

"I have no choice," said Detective Parker. "It's not up for discussion."

Office Boulli started in his chair as if he had been asleep. "But that's not what you said earlier today."

"Officer, be—"

"You said you wanted Miss Webb to help with the investigation. That she would be a great help."

Detective Parker lowered his head in an obvious attempt to control his temper. "You may have been mistaken in what you heard, Officer Boulli." He took a breath and spoke with exaggerated pronunciation. "What I said was that I was disappointed that we could not take advantage of Miss Webb's particular knowledge base until she was cleared."

"I don't remember it that way."

"Then, obviously, you need to work on your listening skills. Paying attention to small details is a critical element for your continued development as an effective officer."

Boulli puffed up and Savannah feared for the health of his shirt buttons. Death by projectile button popped into her head.

The silence lengthened to that uncomfortable state where no one wanted to break it.

Parker's shoulders slumped slightly. "Officer, please check with Coroner Grey about the autopsy report. I'll escort Savannah out of the building."

Officer Boulli's brow furrowed in thought. "But, you just spoke with her on the phone."

"Yes, I did. She said her final report would be ready to pick up right about now. I'd like to have it on my desk by the time I get back."

"Oh, I see." He stood and glared at Savannah, then left the office, propelling his bulk down the hallway at a fast clip.

Savannah pulled her backpack on her shoulder. "He thinks I got him suspended."

"Well, you helped a little. I'm the one who officially submitted the tedious paperwork. He's the reason I am playing by the book. I can't give your innocence the benefit of the doubt. I have to follow the investigative policies and procedures precisely or Officer Boulli will report me to Internal Affairs in a heartbeat."

"So, I'm unofficially innocent but officially a suspect."

"That's about the size of it."

Chapter 16

Savannah drove straight down Central Avenue to 3 Daughters Brewing to meet up with the posse. She couldn't remember if she had invited Keith, so she texted him to meet her there. Her dizzy spell had had no lasting effects other than a residual flush of embarrassment.

Edward stood and waved his whole arm to signal Savannah that the posse had assembled near the foosball game at the back of the brewery. She made her way over to one of the upended wooden cable spools that served for high tops in the large, open warehouse space next to the brightly shining, massive brewing equipment.

"What did you find out?" Amanda panted while desperately spinning the foosball handles forward and backward in wild disorder to defend against Jacob's cool and measured attack. "I lost again?" Her voice registered disbelief as the ball pinged into her goal.

Jacob meticulously adjusted up each paddle bar to straighten each player rod to a perfect vertical, then picked up bootie-less Suzy. "We're awesome at foosball," he whispered into one of her floppy brown ears.

"Hi, guys." Edward motioned to the two pints of beer on the table. "I took the liberty of ordering the Summer Storm Stout for Keith, and, of course, a Beach Blonde Ale for Savannah."

"Thanks"—Keith held up the dark brew—"but I'm strictly an India pale ale man."

Edward quickly swapped his beer with Keith's. "No problem, this is their Bimini Twist IPA. That should work."

Edward looked at Savannah. "What did you discover?"

"Not what we were expecting at all." Savannah took a long sip of her ale. "There's more mystery in this investigation than you can shake a stick at."

"I'll say. At McCloud's"—Keith hopped onto one of the stools—"we were lucky to be there when they found Megan's Best of Show piece stowed in one of the cooling kilns."

Edward scrunched his brow. "Why is that lucky?"

"No one else would have thought to call the police and report it as evidence." Savannah took a long, deep breath. "The resident artists there are so focused on getting as much work done as possible, they're completely single-minded."

Keith sipped his beer. "Good choice, Edward."

He nodded to the pub owner. "I'm so happy that Megan's masterpiece has been found, but it doesn't make sense for it to turn up at McCloud's. I'm completely confused."

"What did Detective Parker think?" asked Edward.

Savannah ducked her head and stared into her drink. "We took the cowards' way out and skulked out of there as soon as they called. I didn't have anything that could help so far, and I really didn't want to discuss my acute lack of ideas with him. Besides, I was scheduled to meet with Detective Parker only a little while after it was discovered. According to procedures, he said he couldn't use me as a consultant as long as I was a suspect."

"That's rubbish," said Edward. "How will we get information to him?"

"Ugh, this is the part that will be awful—he's hired Frank Lattimer as his consultant."

"What? That's crazy. Frank knows nothing about people." Amanda frowned. "Worse, he thinks he has fabulous people skills. He's got nothing. Nothing."

Savannah took a generous swig. "It gets worse. Showing up at the site to discover the missing masterpiece does not look good for my unofficial position on the suspect list either."

Amanda flushed to her spiked hairline. "That's rubbish."

"Speaking of rubbish for ideas"—Edward smiled—"but certainly not lacking in quantity of course, I met with Wanda and had great difficulty getting a word in with dynamite."

Jacob tilted his head. "Why would you use dynamite?"

"Sorry, Jacob, not literally. I meant that she talked so much, it was difficult for me to interrupt her. I did get some answers."

"Well, give, give, give," said Amanda. "We're dying on the vine here."

Still puzzled, Jacob looked at Savannah. She waved a "hold your questions" hand at him. "Spill it, Edward. I need some serious cheering up."

"Maybe this will help. Wanda and Megan did indeed have a loud argument at the reception held the night before the festival. It was over the placement of her booth at the very end of that hidden row. Megan called it 'the row of lost orphans.'"

Amanda giggled. "That's accurate. It was certainly difficult to find—even when you were looking for her booth from the map."

Edward's impatient look silenced Amanda. "Anyway, Megan accused Wanda of being prejudiced against women artists and then Wanda accused Megan of being an entitled spoiled brat."

"Yikes," said Savannah with a frown.

"Megan pointed out that her booth was the last one in the aisle and she also complained to Wanda that most first booths in a row belonged to male artists."

"Jacob, is this true?"

Jacob didn't look up. His gaze moved from

staring at the top of Suzy's head to looking at the foosball paddles and back to Suzy, not touching, just looking. "Yes, Miss Savannah. Of the eighteen aisles, the artists on the end booths are 94.4 percent male."

"After that, it got worse. Megan called Wanda some pretty filthy names. Then, rightly so, Megan was asked to leave the reception."

Savannah held her chin in both hands and propped her elbows on the table. "This is beginning to be useful. Powerful socialite Wanda doesn't want a nobody from out of town to cast doubt on her reputation. That could be a motive."

Edward shook his head negatively. "That's a very weak motive for murder. Irritating as she is, we're talking real violence here. I don't see that."

Finished with staring at the foosball machine, Jacob stood at the spindle table and sipped his root beer. He waited until there was a pause. "I found something, Miss Savannah."

Tilting her head to look at Jacob, she asked, "What?"

"I found an error in the collection of the entry money from the applicants. The money sent in doesn't add up to the prize money documented in the database and given out at the ceremony."

"How big is this error?" Keith asked.

"The difference between the money collected and the money awarded is ten thousand dollars."

"What?" said Edward. "Ten thousand dollars is a lot of money on just the entry fees." He turned to Savannah. "How much is the entry fee?"

Savannah drained her ale. "The jury submission fee is a hundred dollars, and if you are selected, the entry fee is five hundred dollars."

Edward gave a low whistle. "That's a pile of money. That adds up to over a hundred grand in entry fees. How many applicants were there, Jacob?"

"There were 2,053 applications."

Savannah also whistled low. "But almost anyone could have taken the money. There are so many volunteers associated with the running of the Spinnaker Art Festival."

"I have a list." Jacob stretched tall and pulled out a precisely folded sheet of notebook paper from the front pocket of his skinny jeans. "See, I have a list of all the people who could have taken the money. But one of them scores much higher than any of the other volunteers for probability of skimming cash from the festival. I analyzed them and listed them here—all weighted and prioritized with this one at the top of the list."

He gave Savannah the list. "Well, this is a fine mess. The first name on the list is Wanda Quitman."

Amanda slapped her hand on the table. "That's it then. Maybe Megan found out about the skimming and Wanda had to take her out."

"If that's true," Keith said, "she's quite an

actress. During the awards ceremony, I thought her reaction to announcing that Megan was awarded the Best in Show was perfectly genuine. She really looked annoyed. Not the kind of reaction a murderer would have if their victim suddenly ended up in the spotlight."

Savannah frowned. "I agree. I heard her yelp at the announcement. I didn't feel that she was acting at all. Anyway, we need to find out where she was on Saturday night. Edward, are you up for another meeting with Wanda?"

"Really?" His lip curled in an Elvis pout.

A playful smirk tickled Savannah's lips. "It should be easier now that you're under her spell. Please? I'm afraid I'm running out of time with Detective Parker."

Edward grumbled, "I am not a happy bunny."

She batted her eyelashes. "I'll make it up to you, I promise."

"As always, I fall for your womanly wiles. I'll see Wanda."

Savannah turned to Amanda. "Did you find out who was part of Megan's glass team for creating those huge torso pieces?"

"I sorted through more than a hundred pictures on the Duncan McCloud Gallery website and found a shot of the studio with Megan executing one of her pieces. The photos were planned for a lecture to be given at the Museum of Fine Arts next week."

"I'll bet he's scrambling for a replacement," said Keith.

Amanda elbowed him. "Not nice, professor."

Keith rubbed his nudged side. "Sorry, it's just that I feel for him. It's so difficult for these young artists to become as focused on the business side of their craft as they are on the creative side."

"Well, anyway, in the promotional photograph, you can barely see one of the assistants while they're working. Here, I have it right here." She dove an arm into the giant patchwork hobo bag she carried with her. "It's not that clear, but you can see that there are two assistants helping Megan with the torso."

Amanda spread the crumpled computer printout on the wooden surface. "You can only see the side of one of her assistants' faces." She pointed to the image. "It's difficult to tell. It could be Vincent, but it could just as well be Leon."

Savannah turned the print several different directions. "There is only a view of the second assistant's feet. Nothing else."

"Not even enough to identify him or her through unique shoes or clothes. All you can see is a pair of black sneakers and long black jeans. Nothing special."

Jacob piped up, "Leon will know."

"Out of the mouths of babes." Savannah looked at Keith. "We simply must talk to Leon for more information. Good?"

"Yep, I'm good with that."

"Well, I think we've covered all our assignments." Savannah tipped her glass to finish the ale. "Let's review our progress at Webb's tomorrow afternoon. That should give us some time to make things happen. That's all I have. Does anyone else have any further information?"

"I have a question." Jacob bent down to pick up Suzy. "If there are money issues with the collection of artist fees, what about other money that was collected during the festival?"

"Well done, Jacob." Savannah scratched Suzy behind the ears. "A lot of the transactions at the festival were cash. That would be easy to skim."

Edward frowned. "Into the breach with more Wanda schmoozing." He drained his beer in one long swig. "Perfect. Bloody perfect. I'm looking forward to my reward, which I'm declaring right now to be an introduction to my parents. They're arriving on Saturday. Deal?"

"Hmmm . . ." Savannah smiled. "On second thought, I'll go with you. There's no need for you to make such a sacrifice alone." She formed a soft fist and punched him on the shoulder. "No need at all."

Savannah stopped by Webb's before going home. She entered through the back and looked at the whiteboard. Based on the results of everyone so far, she updated the line for Wanda Quitman to indicate a shortage in the entry fees:

The Case of Megan Loyola's Murder

Suspect/Leads	Investigation	Assigned To
Frank Lattimer (S)	Subject of argument at festival	Savannah
Vincent O'Neil (S)	Megan's team member	Savannah
Wanda Quitman (S)	Shortage in entry fees	Edward/ Savannah
Glass shards (L)	Identify origin	Savannah
Registration forms (L)	Find connection patterns in application database	Jacob
Leon Price (S)	Megan's ex-boyfriends	Savannah
Relatives (L)	Research Megan's family	Keith

Standing there in the cozy office, she also thought she needed to do some serious thinking about her feelings toward Edward. He was becoming important to her. Maybe meeting his parents was a good thing. Maybe.

Chapter 17

Wednesday Night

Savannah parked her Mini in the carport of the family's craftsman bungalow. She still considered it to be her dad's home and was happily using her little-girl bedroom with the Jenny Lind spindle twin bed until she decided what to do next. She heard Rooney's "you're home" woof/howl as she walked up the wide porch, with its comfy chairs and porch swing.

"Yoo-hoo, Savannah!" hollered her neighbor across the street, Barbara Webberly. "I'm glad you're finally home."

Savannah flinched at the "finally" but knew that Barbara was absolutely right to comment on her late arrival. Walking over to Mrs. Webberly's front porch, she knew she needed to spend some time with her.

"I took Rooney for a quick walk about an hour ago. I felt so sorry for him."

"Thank you, Mrs. Webberly. I don't know

how Rooney and I would manage without you watching over us." *It annoys me sometimes, but she's got a big heart.*

"I've never minded one whit, honey. Your mother and I were great friends and we had an understanding before she died. I'm keeping my promise. No need to stop now that your dad is gone as well."

What am I thinking? I love Mrs. Webberly.

"You've been a wonderful mother to me, since forever. I'm so grateful." She hugged the yoga-slender form of her surrogate mother and smiled at the warmth of the embrace. Over her shoulder, Savannah noticed that the paint on the front windows was beginning to peel. *I need to give her son a call and tell him about that.*

"Rooney spotted a dark car parked across the street from us and wanted to see who it was. But as soon as they heard him bark, they drove away."

"Strange. Did you see who was in the car?"

"No, it was too dark. Couldn't tell if it was a man or woman. Of course, these days I can't tell that in broad daylight walking down Beach Drive. Anyway, the car was black or navy and looked like every other car on the road. I thought it was strange—thought maybe they were afraid of dogs."

Savannah felt a prickling at the back of her neck. "Maybe. In any case, if the car turns up again, give me a call. I'll let Detective Parker know that there's a suspicious car in my neighborhood.

Thanks." She turned to cross the narrow brick street.

"Oh, just one more thing—Rooney seemed hungry as well, so I fed him his dinner. I hope you don't mind."

"No, of course I don't mind. I appreciate it very much." She watched Mrs. Webberly shuffle next door.

She's getting on in years—soon it will be my turn to take care of her.

She unlocked the door to find Rooney sitting at eager attention to begin their nighttime routine. He bounded into the kitchen and sat by his dinner bowl.

"So you were going to act like you were starving to death and let me feed you a second supper?" He responded by pushing the empty bowl toward her feet.

Rooney tilted his head and gave her puppy eyes. She melted and indulged in a rough-and-tumble followed by belly rubs that left her giggling at Rooney's pleasure growls. "You have me wrapped around your giant paws."

She let him out the back door and they concentrated on agility drills for the next half hour. When his attention started to wander, they went back into the kitchen for a reward of dog biscuits followed by another hug and tickle fest.

Curious about the car Mrs. Webberly mentioned, Savannah peeked out the front window and saw a dark car parked across the street a few houses down the block. "Come, Rooney." She grabbed his leash and snapped it to his collar;

then they stepped out onto the porch. As soon as Rooney got a good whiff of the evening air, he howled bloody murder. The car pulled out sharply and spun tires down the street.

"Stay, Rooney." She struggled to keep him from chasing the car down the street. "No, no, no. No chasing cars for you." Since they were already out and leashed, she took Rooney up and down the street on the chance that the car might come back. Without a license plate number there was nothing to tell anyone. After three circuits of the block, they stood on the front porch for a few minutes. "Okay, Rooney, we're done. Bad guys are gone."

She went back inside, locked the front door, unleashed Rooney, and walked into the kitchen. She opened the freezer door and stood in front of her selection of frozen meals. The single servings reminded her that she had promised to do some serious thinking to sort out her feelings about Edward. She knew she wasn't the single-serving type. Family was important to her, even here alone in her family home.

Edward was so different from her ex-boyfriend back in Seattle. So different that it was possibly too good to be true. Her ex-boyfriend had turned out to be needy, whiney, and in the end completely incapable of seeing her as anything but an extension of his wants and needs. That he turned out to be such a disaster rocked her confidence.

Just as she was pulling out a somewhat healthy frozen meal for the microwave, the doorbell rang and Rooney barked a warning.

Looking through the peephole, she saw Keith standing on her porch with both hands holding reusable grocery bags. She unlocked the door. "Keith, what are you doing here?"

Rooney stopped barking and stood quietly by Savannah's side.

"You haven't eaten yet, have you?" Keith bolted through the door and stood looking at her with a wide, mischievous grin.

"No, but I was about to—"

"Don't tell me. Let me guess. Frozen dinner, right?"

Savannah frowned. "What's wrong with that? They are simple and perfect for—"

"Someone who lives alone. I know that all too well. Anyway, I'm here to cook us a fabulous meal in minutes."

"But—"

"Nothing doing. I'll only be fifteen minutes. I found fresh flounder at that new market downtown and I have a great recipe. You have an oven, right?"

"Yes, of course there's an oven." *Thank goodness I got a cleaning service. Everything is reasonably clean and tidy thanks to their weekly visits.* "The kitchen is right through here."

"Wow, I didn't expect such a modern kitchen."

He looked around at the industrial six-burner stove, the deep white farm sink, a sizable worktable with a butcher-block surface, and the hanging rack of stainless steel pots along with well-used iron skillets that were seasoned to a glistening black. "Your dad must have loved to cook."

"He did," said Savannah. "I don't cook much, but I know how to make excellent reservations."

Keith laughed. "I thought as much." He looked out the back door at the agility course. "What's that? Are you doing one of those athletic team competitions?"

"No, that's for Rooney. We practice a little in the backyard every day. It's good for him and burns off his energy."

He looked at the magnetic rack of knives mounted over the stove. "Oh, fantastic. Knives, real-quality knives. I'm in love." He put the groceries down on the butcher-block worktable. "If you'll set up the dining table for us, I'll get cracking. Oh, send in the dinner plates. I want to preheat them."

"I've got a Pinot Grigio that might go well with the flounder." She showed the bottle to Keith. "Good?"

"Perfect. Now out. I can find whatever I need. Out."

Savannah removed her mother's china and silverware from the antique oak cabinet in the dining room, wiped them with a dish towel, and then gave Keith the plates. By the time she arranged two place settings, put four white candles in her grandmother's cut-glass candelabra, opened the white wine, and poured two glasses, Keith was ready with their grilled fish, a side of roasted broccolini, and toasted garlic bread. She lit the candles and enjoyed the idea of a relaxing evening.

The fish was perfect. The bread and broccolini were perfect. Rooney was behaving nicely under the table. The wine and especially the company were perfect.

It's very nice to be looked after. Is that what I'm looking for? Maybe it's time to look to the future.

"That certainly passed the silence test." Keith downed the last sip of his wine.

"Silence test?"

"It's a compliment to the food that no one spoke a word during the meal." She looked down and was shocked to see a clean plate. He poured more wine into her glass and the rest of the bottle went into his.

"It was fantastic and I was simply famished. Thanks for cooking for me."

"Well, now that you are no longer my student . . ."

Savannah looked down into her wineglass and swirled its contents. *This is getting a little too cozy for me.* She cut him off. "What did you think of Mcgan's talent?"

Keith drank more wine and sat back in his chair. He took a great long breath. "I thought she was a bright girl trying very, very hard to impress her unimpressible parents by blazing a fast track through the art world."

"What were her earlier pieces like?"

He rubbed his face and leaned back. "Sadly, unremarkable. But each of her relationships seemed to make a difference in her work—passion followed by agony followed by a new passion. There's no use trying to make art through someone else's vision—you must have your own heart in your work."

"I think with this last exhibit she found her heart, literally and figuratively," said Savannah.

"I agree with you about the works she exhibited at the festival—they were undeniably the work of a passionate heart."

"Do you think it represents a heart that finally found true love?"

Keith swirled the last of his wine and drained the glass. "That is possible, but it would be more likely that she rekindled a prior love. Remember one of my adages about behavior?"

"Yes, yes. 'The best predictor of future behavior is past behavior.' I remember that too well. But I don't think her new work is based on her typical string of exploited lovers. I think this is something new. I think she found someone she loved and the centerpiece was the image of that love. Do you know who it was?"

Keith stood. "No, no clue at all. Well, due to lack of wine and the late hour, I'm going to call an end to this lovely evening." He gave Savannah a chaste peck on the cheek and was out the door.

Watching his car pull away, Savannah felt a little abandoned. Not that she wanted to encourage anything with her former mentor, but he was a good-looking man with a track record for launching careers.

Rooney nuzzled her knee and looked up at her with hopeful eyes. "Okay, luv. I'll take you for a quick walk. Luv? Where did that come from? I'm beginning to sound like Edward."

Chapter 18

Thursday Morning

At dawn, Savannah and Rooney hurried through their morning routine of wolfing down a hearty breakfast, slipping into running clothes, putting on his running leash, then driving down to Coffee Pot Bayou Park in the Northeast section of St. Petersburg. They started out at the boat ramp at the top end of Coffee Pot Boulevard NE. Rooney wriggled pure joy as they began running down the sidewalk bordered by Tampa Bay on one side and the elitist Old Northeast mansions on the other.

"It's good to be back to a normal routine, isn't it, Rooney?"

Rooney was loping along, eyes alert and ears perked, not yet even breathing with his mouth open. They covered the first two miles easily and began the stretch that runs parallel to where the Spinnaker Art Festival committee's mobile office trailer had been. Only a set of deep wheel ruts gave any hint of its former location.

Looking down at Rooney she said, "You're very serious this morning. What has gotten your—"

Whoosh! A dark hoodie-clad figure oozing a familiar scent bolted out of nowhere and grabbed Savannah by the right arm. Rooney responded with panicked barking while the attacker shoved her roughly toward the seawall. In the corner of her eye, she could see the water glinting with the morning sun.

Fearing that she would bash her head on the concrete seawall and then drown, she could feel the sound of her heartbeat thrashing a rapid pulse.

Letting loose with an ear-splitting scream, Savannah slumped down into a tuck position and rolled away from her assailant. That left him facing a bristling Rooney, who had turned into a snarling mass of anger. As the attacker turned to run away, Rooney snagged the black trousers and the attacker fell onto his knee with a painful yelp. It was over in a second. When Savannah struggled to her feet, all she had left to prove she had been attacked was a deep scrape on her leg and a small scrap of dark material that Rooney was holding in his mouth as she shook like a rag doll.

Trembling from head to foot, Savannah limped over to plop breathless on the nearest park bench, then examined the bleeding scrape.

I'm safe.

She looked at Rooney, who, puppy-like, had moved to sit beside her and looked ready to continue their run.

No experienced mugger would have attacked her with Rooney running by her side. This must have had a greater purpose—maybe she had finally stepped on someone's toes with her investigation. Progress at last, but at what cost?

She realized she had to tell Detective Parker about the latest developments. She took out her cell phone, which she carried with her during Rooney's walks, and dialed his direct extension.

"Homicide, Detective Parker."

"Hi, this is Savannah Webb. I've been—"

"I'm not available just now. My office hours are from eight A.M. to five P.M., Monday through Friday. If this is an emergency, please dial nine-one-one; otherwise, leave a message. Beep."

"Good morning, Detective Parker. This is Savannah Webb and I want to report an incident that may relate to Megan Loyola's murder. Someone tried to pitch me over the seawall on my training run this morning. I'm not really hurt, only a scrape, so this isn't an emergency. Anyway, he was wearing a black hoodie and jeans, so I have no description other than I thought it was a man. Please call me on my cell. You have the number from my statement. Bye."

Savannah pressed the END CALL button and slipped the phone back into her running shorts pocket and pulled the zipper shut. "I forgot it was so early, Rooney boy." She reached for the scrap that Rooney held. He playfully twirled away like a game of tag. "No, Rooney, this is not a game. Stay!"

Rooney stopped in his tracks, then sat with his forepaws extended waiting for her next move.

Savannah tried to calm the fluttering feeling in her belly. She must be unintentionally telling Rooney that this was a play game.

"Good boy. Good boy, Rooney." She crept up to him and slowly reached for the leash. Just as her hands were within an inch of grabbing it, he danced away tossing the scrap and catching it in midair. "Rooney, stay!"

He froze into a sitting position. "Stay, Rooney. Good boy." This time she put her hand out in front of his nose and looked him in the eyes with a frightening glare. It worked. She picked up his leash and gently removed the sopping wet scrap of fabric from his mouth. "Good Rooney," she baby-talked. "He's a good boy! Yes, such a good boy!"

Rooney squirmed puppy delight from his nose to the tip of his tail. She placed the torn scrap in one of Rooney's scooper bags and tied it to the leash handle.

She breathed in a few long, slow breaths and felt the calmness making a small stand against the aftermath of the attack. One thing she was certain about: she wasn't going to tell her posse. They would insist on her stopping the investigation. Not that they wouldn't be right, but she really wanted to find the killer.

She looked down at her leg and the scrape had bled a half-inch red streak down into her white running sock but hadn't reached her new white Skechers. She kicked off her shoes, removed the clean sock, and pressed it against the scrape to stop the bleeding.

At least I've ruined a matching pair.

Looking to her left, she didn't see anyone suspicious. Whoever attacked her either had a car nearby or parked near one of the manicured backyards of the mansions close by. That was the safer bet as most of their unimaginably rich owners spent only the winter months of January through March indulging in the mild climate. Now that it was well into April they had flown back north. That was why the locals called them snowbirds. Their tourist dollars supported the city's economy and provided desperately needed funding for the city's charities.

On her right, however, was a more likely escape route through the thick foliage of the Gizella Kopsick Palm Arboretum. Although a fascinating collection of every type of palm capable of growing in the climate, it was typically deserted and provided lots of cover for an escaping assailant.

Her pulse had finally returned to a resting rate. "Rooney, I've been silly. I hate that. This was probably a normal snatch and grab from someone who thought I was an easy mark. It has nothing to do with Megan."

It's not all about you, Savannah. I wish I hadn't called Parker.

Lifting the sock away from the scrape, she confirmed that the bleeding had stopped. She removed the blood-soaked sock and placed both in another of Rooney's scooper bags.

She stood and tested the injured leg. A little pain, but no muscle strain or fresh bleeding. Savannah and Rooney walked at a limping pace back to the Mini.

"Okay, Rooney, let's get home so I can dress this scrape. I don't think it will stop us from entering you in the agility competition on Saturday, but I'd better take care of it sooner rather than later. It is pretty ugly."

She removed the leash and its little evidence parcel, then clipped Rooney into his car seat on the passenger side of the Mini. As he did every single time, he whined and looked at her as if she were condemning him to life in prison, but finally curled up and she drove home.

Once inside, she refreshed his water bowl, showered, bandaged her scrape properly, and got changed for work in her normal workday outfit of jeans and a collared golf shirt with the Webb's Glass Shop logo. As she was picking up her keys, her cell phone rang. The caller ID announced PARKER SPPD.

"Hello."

"Savannah, this is Detective Parker. I got your message. What is this about an attack?"

"Yes, this morning near the place where I found Megan's body."

"Why didn't you call nine-one-one?"

"It wasn't an emergency. I don't need medical assistance. I don't even have a decent description except that he was wearing black jeans and a black hoodie. Not too helpful."

"Let me be the judge of that. I still need a statement, so I'll come by the shop this morning. Next time, call nine-one-one or an on-duty officer. Don't just leave a message on my machine."

"I apologize. You're absolutely right. I'll be at the shop in about fifteen minutes."

"Good."

During the short drive to the shop, Savannah considered her actions regarding the attack. Should she be concerned that it might be connected with the investigation or was it an ordinary mugging? It seemed an odd time for a mugging and, in any case, most joggers don't carry wallets. Even more frightening, muggers don't usually attack joggers with dogs.

If he knew I would be jogging there, has he been following me? Maybe that's who Mrs. Webberly saw in the strange car.

She pulled around to the back of the shop and found Detective Parker waiting for her with a takeaway tray holding two coffees and a bag of Krispy Kreme donuts.

"Detective, I thought *I* was supposed to bribe *you* with coffee and donuts," she said as she locked the Mini. "I'm pleased to be on the receiving end of such a stereotypical graft."

He laughed in a deep, rich tone that sounded practiced. She unlocked the door, tapped the code into the alarm system, and motioned Detective Parker into a side chair. "I need to make a quick call and then we'll talk about the attack."

Savannah speed dialed Edward and left a voice mail: "Morning, Edward, I've already got my early coffee. I'll see you later on when the posse gets together, okay? Great."

"Posse?"

"Um . . . that's what I call my little investigation team."

Detective Parker shook his head slowly from side to side. "I can't condone this, Savannah. I caution you that you're playing a dangerous game."

"Do you think that's why I was attacked this morning? Someone who may be worried that I'm getting too close for their safety? Isn't that a sign of progress?"

"I want you to stop investigating, *especially* if it's putting you in danger."

"Now that I've started, I'm going to continue until Megan's killer is revealed."

"But why? You know I don't think it's you."

"It's a little hard to explain, but she was living the life I would have had if my dad hadn't died and I had stayed in Seattle. I feel close to her."

"Can you at least share your progress with me?"

"Of course." Savannah sipped her coffee and looked beyond Detective Parker's shoulder at the whiteboard.

Following her gaze, Detective Parker twisted

in his chair. He stood and laughed. "You are something. If you were my assistant instead of Officer Boulli, I have the feeling that this murderer would have been found already." He squinted at the board. "Why is Frank's name up there? What argument?"

"Several of the artists on the same row with Megan's booth said that she and Frank had an intense argument right before the festival ended on Saturday. It was right before I came by and she was still upset. She wouldn't tell me what upset her, but we're trying to find out. I told Frank to call you. He's supposed to be your technical adviser."

"And you can see how well that is working out. Having another expert end up on the suspect list would be a major blow to the investigation."

"Anyway, Frank says it has nothing to do with Megan's death."

He turned around. "Seriously now. What do you remember about the attack this morning?"

"Not much. I was thinking about Megan and trying to figure out why someone would want to kill her when someone grabbed my arm and tried to shove me over the seawall." She rubbed her left arm and looked at the darkening bruise. "Great, that's going to turn ugly. Anyway, Rooney grabbed his jeans and scared him away."

"I'm surprised he tried to attack you while Rooney was running with you."

Savannah shrugged her shoulders. "Why would he attack me in the first place?"

"You keep referring to your attacker as male. What is making you think that?"

"Good question. I think it was the strength of the push. There's something else, but I can't remember. It will come to me."

"Call me when it does." He took out one of his business cards and wrote on the back. "Next time you don't think you're having an emergency, call my private cell." He handed it to Savannah. "This is probably not the last time he will try to discourage you from the investigation."

She tucked the card into her back jeans pocket. "Oh, I almost forgot." She reached into her backpack and pulled out Rooney's scooper bag. "Rooney tore a hunk of material from the attacker's pants. I had to touch it to get it away from Rooney, so that scrap should have the attacker's DNA along with mine and Rooney's, of course. Do you need a DNA sample from Rooney?"

Detective Parker chuckled. "No, the forensics lab will be able to tell the difference."

Chapter 19

Thursday Morning

After seeing Detective Parker pull away, Savannah went back to her office and stood in front of the board with both hands on her hips. Why had he laughed when he looked at it? Had she written something stupid up there?

She made her way through the classroom and into the display and retail room to boot up the register, unlock the front door, and then turn her sign from CLOSED to OPEN. No sooner had she returned to the display counter to confirm that the computer was ready than Jacob hustled inside the door out of breath.

"Miss Savannah, I found the missing student."

"What?"

Jacob shifted his weight from one foot to the other. "I found the missing student."

"How did you do that?"

"I listed the addresses of the applicants who filled out the form as students. They pay a reduced fee, so they have to fill in the name of the school and send in a scan of their picture identification.

"I found that the out-of-area students find lodging at eight different places that rent by the week. I asked my mother to call them and ask to speak to Vincent O'Neil."

Of course, he doesn't use the phone. I'm glad his mother and I talked about his research.

"That was clever." She smiled. "Go on, then what?"

"No one was registered by that name, so I had my father call again and ask for a variation using his middle name, Vincent Henry." Jacob smiled wide.

"So, what happened?"

"We found him working as a maintenance man at The Pier Hotel, which has given him an employee weekly rate and is within walking distance of the festival."

"That is super awesome." Savannah reached out to hug him and remembered in time not to touch him. She awkwardly waved her arms in a big circle. "Edward and I will talk to him today."

"I had another plan for my mother to call and ask for Henry O'Neil. I didn't have to use that plan."

Savannah grinned. "Asking a judge to lie— you might have gotten into trouble with that plan."

"My dad asked if he was home. The desk manager said he had very odd hours. He works at the Chihuly Museum. After it closes he goes to work at a studio late at night until dawn."

"Okay, that's going to make things harder. Thanks for tracking him down."

The front door jangled as Amanda entered the shop. "Hey, guys. You look cheery. What's up?"

Savannah folded her arms. "Jacob found our missing student, Vincent. That means you are going to be teaching class this morning."

"But—" Amanda's naturally pale face turned a shade whiter. "I'm not ready to teach yet. I'm supposed to shadow you this whole week."

"Murder changes everyone's plans. Don't worry, you are ready." Savannah gave her a big hug. "I wouldn't leave you in charge of Webb's if I wasn't completely confident in your abilities, would I? You know how much I treasure its reputation."

"That's true." Amanda's shoulders relaxed a bit. "Today's pretty easy; it's emptying the kiln and getting things ready for loading it up again for tonight's fusing."

"See, you're completely ready for this. Everything you need to know is in my lesson plan on the podium. You're going to be great."

Savannah pulled out her cell phone and dialed Edward. "Hey! Are you able to get away for a bit? Jacob located Vincent, and he's at The Pier Hotel downtown."

"Now?"

"Yep, now. Meet me out back. I'll drive."

"Give me a couple of minutes to call in an additional server."

"Of course."

Savannah waved bye to Amanda and Jacob,

then grabbed her backpack and went out and unlocked the Mini in time for Edward to slip into the passenger seat. "I want to get to Vincent before he disappears again. He's registered by using his middle name as his last name." She drove the Mini downtown and found a space in The Pier Hotel's parking lot.

Edward hopped out of the car. "Who brought your coffee this morning? It couldn't have been as good as mine."

"Hmmm, it wasn't. But I'm not silly enough to annoy Detective Parker. Especially when he's trying to keep me out of jail."

"Why did he stop by the shop himself? He could have sent Officer Boulli."

"Apparently Boulli is holding a grudge against me for causing his suspension. He might not report the actual facts in my favor."

Savannah turned to Edward, knowing that she should tell him about the attack this morning. She thought about how he might react. Would he get possessive? Would he try to control her? Would he get angry?

I'm not willing to find out.

They looked up at the façade of the turn-of-the-century traditional Florida tourist hotel.

"This has been here a long time." Savannah and Edward walked under the long white awning that covered the length of the entry sidewalk to the salmon pink hotel. They walked up the chipped concrete steps and stepped onto a broad old-fashioned veranda filled with white wicker chairs and greenery hanging from the porch ceiling and in white wicker planters. Edward opened the front door and let Savannah through to the lobby. "My house was built at about the same time as this." She looked at the lobby/sitting room furnished with comfort inducing plush carpeting, oak-colored grand piano, and a large fireplace.

Walking up to the registration counter, Savannah asked the elderly clerk, "Would you please tell Vincent Henry that his visitors are in the lobby?"

"Yes, ma'am. It would be my pleasure."

Smiling at the genuine southern drawl, Savannah dragged Edward over to a seating area to the side of the lobby that was not immediately visible to a guest coming down to the area. "Let's wait over here." They plopped down onto a comfortable velvet settee.

A slim, wiry young man with sandy hair tied into a short ponytail walked into the lobby and leaned over the registration counter. "You said I had visitors?"

The clerk used his black pen to point at Savannah and Edward at the other end of the lobby. He walked over to them with his brow furrowed. "Do I know you?"

Savannah stood and extended her hand. "No, Vincent, but we're here to help you. I'm Savannah Webb, owner of Webb's Glass Shop and recent judge of the Spinnaker Art Festival." She turned slightly to Edward. "This is my good friend, Edward Morris. He's the owner of Queen's Head Pub."

Vincent crossed his arms over his chest. "Why are you here?"

"We have some questions for you about Megan." Savannah motioned to the seat across from them. "Please have a seat and let's talk."

"How did you find me?" He held his head in both hands. "Oh no, if you found me then anyone can." He put his hands to his mouth and turned a shade paler. "How did you find me?"

Edward put a hand on Vincent's shoulder. "Calm down, buddy. Our friend Jacob found you with a few lucky guesses. He has amazing intuitive skills, and relentless determination. I don't think anyone else will bother." He gently pulled Vincent over to the overstuffed chair at a right angle to their settee. "Relax. Sit."

Savannah leaned forward. "I found Megan's body on Monday morning and I'm working with the police to catch her killer. We need your help."

"I moved here to the hotel as soon as I heard about her murder." Vincent looked at Edward, rubbed his trembling hands together, then leaned back and folded his arms across his body.

Edward glanced at Savannah and she nodded slightly for him to talk. "You were one of her studio assistants, right?"

"Yeah, she was really particular about who worked with her." Vincent looked directly at Edward. "The pieces she made were extremely difficult and took multiple sessions to complete. In fact, I don't think I've ever worked on anything so complicated."

"When did you see her last?" Savannah softened her voice. "Was it at the festival?"

Vincent glanced quickly at Savannah, but turned to Edward. "Yes, I saw her at her booth pretty much the first thing on Saturday morning. Her booth was spectacular. Did you see it?"

Edward silently shook his head. "Why didn't you have a booth?"

Vincent sighed deeply. "My work isn't ready yet. I'm almost there, but not quite." He coughed and rubbed his forearms briskly. "It's hard to be almost there. I don't feel I can show my work until the process is perfected. That was Megan's approach and it worked like magic."

"What technique are you working on?" asked Savannah.

Leaning back with a broad smile he continued to answer to Edward. "I'm dabbling with Buddhist forms using colored sand castings. I'm working on using naturally colored sands to enhance the expressions on the Buddha's face. I've been collecting different colored sands all over the world." He looked down into his spread hands. "I'm almost there."

Edward looked like he was trying to imagine sand in Buddha's face. He shook his head to rid it of the distracting image. "Where were you on Saturday night?"

He stood up abruptly. "I didn't kill Megan! I was working at the Chihuly Museum during my regular shift until eight; then I went to my studio and worked until about two in the morning."

"Can anyone verify that?" Savannah posed gently.

"No." Vincent plopped back down into the chair. "No one. But I think I know who the killer is and I think he's coming after me next."

"Who is it?" Savannah asked.

Vincent looked at Savannah with a mixture of fear and revulsion. She thought that some woman in his past had been very cruel to him for him to react so oddly to her. She looked over to Edward and tilted her head toward Vincent.

Edward got the message. "Who is it?"

"I don't think I should say. She'll know—" Vincent stood for a moment, then started for his room.

Edward and Savannah looked at each other and mouthed *She?* at the same time.

Edward grabbed Vincent by the arm. "You need to tell us. You won't be safe until she is caught."

Savannah stood. "You need to tell the police so they can stop her threats to your safety. That's the only logical way. You know that."

"Sometimes logic has nothing to do with real life. I intend to keep mine."

"Give us a hint. Something. If you don't, you're going to stay on the list as a suspect. Tell us where you were and we'll work it out with Detective Parker."

He paused for a measured moment. "Okay, I've already moved from there, so I can tell you.

It's a collection of hot glass artists who share workspace in the warehouse district. It's in Gulfport in the Industrial Arts Center. But, no one will be able to confirm that I was there. Most of them work there during the day. I work there at night because no one is around."

"You never know." Savannah pulled a business card from her backpack. "Here, if something comes up and you want to talk, give me a call."

Looking down at the card and back to Edward, he said, "I'm not planning to talk to anyone. That way I'll stay safe. Now, go away."

Chapter 20

After leaving The Pier Hotel, Savannah pulled into an available parking space in front of the Museum of Fine Arts and across from the Chihuly Museum on Beach Drive. Digging into her cup holder for the hoard of change she kept there, she said, "Let's eat. I'm starved."

Edward watched her feed the meter enough coins to max out the time to two hours. "Are you planning to camp out here? Two hours is way more than lunch."

"I always max it out. That means someone else gets a free hour or more and it's a nice way to get rid of change. Otherwise, I think I'd be knee-deep in silver coins."

Edward chuckled and shook his head. "What do you do with the pennies?"

"Oh, those I donate to The Guide Dog Charity using one of those coin-counter machines at the Publix grocery store."

"That's good—much better than the pickle jar I have full of coins."

They crossed busy Beach Drive, Edward holding Savannah by the hand. "Where do you want to eat?"

She scanned the outdoor tables along the street. "How about The Canopy? It's out of the pedestrian traffic and I love the view of the city."

"Sure, but it's pricey."

"My treat. Say, how are things at Queen's Head? Have the breakfast hours helped with revenue?"

"In the very first week, the new breakfast hour broke even, and I should be able to hire another server next week to give me and Nicole a break. Since we've only been at it this week, that's a good sign that we'll be keeping it going."

They took the elevator to the fourth-floor open-air deck of the Birchwood Hotel. They perched onto bar stools pulled up to a high-top table that overlooked the bay and their waiter took an order for a plate of Chicken-Fried Calamari and the Coast to Coast Artisanal Cheese Plate along with a glass of house red each.

Edward fidgeted in his seat after they ordered and looked like he was about to burst if something didn't get said.

"Out with it," she said. "What is it you want to say?"

Their server walked up with the wine and he waited until he left.

"I wanted to make sure you're . . ."

"I'm what?"

"That you're fine with my folks coming. They really want to meet you and I don't want you to misunderstand that this could be a sort of formal commitment. You know, the dreaded meeting-the-parents ordeal."

"Don't worry, Edward. Really, I'm fine. I'm sure it will be fine. To family."

They clinked their glasses and sipped the wine.

Savannah pulled out her phone. "This restaurant is quiet enough for me to call Detective Parker."

"You aren't going to wait for Vincent to call?"

"I don't think there's a snowball's chance in hell that he'll call. He's a pretty strange character, even for an artist. Besides, he wouldn't even look at me. Can you imagine him calling Detective Parker, or me? No way!"

She reached him at his office number. "Hi, this is Savannah Webb. My apprentice, Jacob, was able to use the artist applications to get a location for the missing student, Vincent O'Neil. I'm with Edward downtown and I'm putting you on speaker."

She pressed the speaker button and placed the phone on their table. "He's staying at The Pier Hotel, but we may have spooked him."

"You went over to talk to him?"

"He seemed very nervous and didn't want to talk to—"

"Hey! There's Vincent." Edward stood and leaned over the glass barrier. "He's meeting someone. I can't tell who it is from the top. Can you?"

"Sorry, I gotta go." She ended the call and Savannah looked down and spotted Vincent down the street on the corner of Beach Drive and Third Avenue North, a block away from the Chihuly Museum.

"No, it's too far." She squinted and shielded her eyes with her hand. "This angle is impossible. It might be anyone."

"Let's find out."

"Right." She lifted up her backpack and pulled out her billfold to pay for their drinks.

"Never mind. They've separated and it looks like Vincent is going into work."

"Where's the stranger?"

"Getting into that black car over there." Edward pointed to a late-model generic-looking car. "The car is going to drive by us."

Savannah pulled a pair of binoculars from a side pocket of her backpack and focused them on the driver. "Okay, I got it. Oh my goodness!"

"Who is it?"

She lowered the binoculars. "It's Wanda Quitman."

Edward shook his head and raised an eyebrow. "That doesn't make any sense, does it? Why would a festival coordinator be talking to an artist from out of town who didn't even make the cut to have a booth?"

"Maybe she's the 'she' that Vincent thinks killed Megan and is out to kill him. I don't know. It gets more and more confusing." She looked back toward the elevator. "I need to eat but I'd better call Detective Parker back and update him. He's definitely going to give me another lecture. This would be so much easier if I had a viable theory for Megan's murder."

"Don't panic just yet. We still have a ton of leads to follow."

"I know." She propped her elbow on the table and rested her forehead in her palm. "I'm so frustrated. So far, all our answers don't result in anything but more questions."

Edward rubbed the knot that bunched in Savannah's neck. "Calm down and call Parker. The news won't get any better by delaying it."

"Yep," Savannah said as she dialed.

"Detective Parker, Homicide."

"This is Savannah. Sorry for the disconnect. We just saw Vincent meet with Wanda Quitman in front of the Chihuly Museum, but—"

The phone went silent for several seconds.

"Hang on," followed by silence—a long silence. Savannah held her breath.

"Detective Parker, are you there?"

More silence.

She took a look at the display on her phone, shook the phone, and looked at Edward. "I think the call has been dropped. I haven't had a dropped call in ages. It—"

"I'm here." Detective Parker clipped the words sharply. "I'm here. I was getting my file. What student are you talking about?"

"I'm putting you on speaker. Edward is here with me."

"Fine, fine."

"When Megan came to St. Petersburg, she was

one of three students from the Pilchuck Glass School. Two of them received grants to intern at the Chihuly Museum. Leon was one of them and his work was exhibited in the same aisle with Megan, but Vincent's work didn't get committee approval."

"Okay, so this is the third student from Seattle?"

"Yes, Keith couldn't locate him right after Megan was killed. He was hiding in plain sight working at the Chihuly Museum under a variation of his real name. His alias is Vincent Henry, but his real name is Vincent O'Neil. He lives at The Pier Hotel in exchange for maintenance work so he's not registered as a regular guest, but Jacob found him."

"Jacob, of course. I wish we had a Jacob on the force." He paused. "Okay, our investigation was very close behind Jacob and we probably would have gotten there sometime tomorrow or the next day."

"I'm sure Vincent knows something about Megan's death that he wouldn't tell me. He referred to the killer as a she."

Parker's voice pitched high. "You've talked to him?"

"Well, I wanted to make sure we were on the right track. Jacob came up with a list of seven artists calculated by different probabilities—all weighted and prioritized, with Vincent O'Neil at the top of his list."

"You could have given me the names. We

should have confirmed them. It would have been, perhaps, safer for you and your little posse."

"But—"

"No buts."

"But—"

"Savannah. Listen carefully. I want you to stop investigating Megan's murder. I don't think that attack this morning was a random mugging. If you keep poking around, it's going to get you in trouble."

"I'm already in trouble."

"What? Has something else happened since this morning?"

"No, no. Another thing that Jacob discovered is that there is a lot of cash missing from the proceeds of the Spinnaker Art Festival. At least ten grand and probably a lot more since the beer and wine sales are mostly cash."

"That's a serious charge. Does he have proof?"

"No—he has the data from the records I was able to get him from my account as a Spinnaker judge."

"Is there anything else you think I might need to know?"

"No, but I'm still a suspect, aren't I?"

Silence.

"Aren't I?"

"Yes, but that's merely a formality."

"But I'm still on the list."

"No one is actively investigating you right now."

"Okay, I understand."

"The point is that investigating a murder is

dangerous and you could get hurt. Worse, one of the members in your posse could get hurt. Have you thought of how you would feel if something happened to Jacob or Edward?"

Savannah looked at Edward. "I haven't—"

"Exactly my point. Stop investigating. If I catch you, I will charge you with interfering with an ongoing investigation or perhaps obstruction of justice. In fact, if you so much as litter or jaywalk, I'm going to put you in a holding cell. Have I made myself clear?"

Nodding at the phone, she replied, "Yes, very clear."

She heard a clunk followed by the dial tone and imagined a very annoyed Detective Parker slamming down his desk receiver.

"He's not taking this very well, is he?"

"Not as grateful as I would have expected."

Edward grinned. "I'm not sure how grateful I'd feel if you were doing my job better than me at every turn. If fact, I'd be well put out."

Savannah stuck out her tongue.

"No wonder he wants to arrest you for jaywalking."

"Never mind that. We've got to figure out what's next. I think a regrouping is in order. Let's round up the posse this afternoon and brainstorm our next steps."

Edward looked at his watch. "Can we do that at about four? I've got some vendor calls to make this afternoon. Unfortunately, we need a new bakery supplier and I've got to do that quickly.

In fact, I'm already in trouble—most of them close at around now."

"Right, I'll drop you off in front of your motorcycle. Good, here comes our food. I'm starved."

After leaving Edward, Savannah drove south on Twenty-Second Street to find the studio space that Vincent mentioned. She parked across the street from a single-story building painted the ugliest shade of burnt ochre ever invented.

Wandering around the back side of the mustard monstrosity to the demonstration area, she came upon a group sitting by the hot glass furnace. They were in the planning stages of a new piece and were making sketches of a vase.

"Excuse me, but do any of you know Vincent Henry O'Neil? I think he works here at night. He makes glass castings in sand."

A wiry woman looked up from the sketch. "You mean Henry? The one who casts Buddha heads?"

"Buddha heads. Yes, that's the one. Have any of you seen him lately?"

"Not lately. He works real late at night. Alone." The woman stood and put her hands on her hips. "Why? What's he done?"

"Nothing, I'm trying to reach him to offer him a place at my new studio." She handed the woman one of the new business cards she had made for Webb's Studio. "If you see him, can you give him this?"

The woman took the card and turned it over in her hands. "I'll put it up on the message board, but if you really want to see him come down here after midnight." She walked over to the left-hand wall and pinned the card to a corkboard over-stuffed with notes, cards, a single athletic sock, and advertisements for items for sale with telephone numbers ready to tear away.

Savannah nodded thanks and left. *Why would someone leave a sock in a studio?*

Chapter 21

At Webb's, Savannah slipped in through the back door and dropped her backpack on the floor beside the creaky oak desk chair. She stepped into the doorway that led to the classroom and found Amanda standing behind the instructor podium grasping the sides with white-knuckled hands.

"Amanda?" She walked up and waved a hand in front of her chalky white face to break the frozen expression. "Amanda, what's wrong?"

"It's broken."

"What?"

"My favorite dish. He broke it." Amanda gathered up the pieces from the top shelf of the podium to show Savannah.

Savannah looked at the pieces cradled in Amanda's hands. "Who broke it?"

"Dale dropped it," burbled from a throat ready to throw up. "I know it was an accident, but I'm—"

"I know, you're very upset." Savannah patted her on the shoulder and looked at the damage. The fused platter had split into four pieces, all of which were along the fused seams where the different colors met.

As Savannah looked at the pieces, it brought back a memory of her teenaged self crying over another broken platter. In a soothing tone, she said, "You know we can fix this."

Amanda looked up with eyes that threatened to spill heavy tears. "We can?"

"Sure we can. That was one of the first things my dad taught me about fused glass. He found me crying over one of my early efforts as well." She smiled remembering his calm, measured advice. "Lay out the pieces over here on this worktable."

After gingerly placing the pieces on the surface, Amanda stepped back and looked at Savannah like a puppy expecting a treat. "Now what?"

Gently pushing the pieces back together, she said, "Go get the mold you used for this piece." Amanda took off like a shot for the display room shelves. Savannah spread the pieces out a bit, then lifted her voice. "Grab one that's a size larger, too."

When Amanda returned with the two molds, Savannah took the smaller one and placed the pieces in it. "Look, the pieces all fit nicely in the original mold and we can fuse it again to get a new dish."

Her face returning to its normal pale shade, Amanda said, "I would never have thought of that. I was going to scrap the whole thing."

"Another approach would be to take the larger mold, select a complementary background color, and arrange the broken pieces for the best effect." She moved them around in several configurations.

"Wow." Amanda's voice was clear and cheerful. "I like that."

"You need to remember rule number one for fusing glass. It's 'Never refuse to re-fuse.'"

"That's funny."

"But easy to remember." Savannah patted her on the shoulder. "This one would be a rebirth of your favorite dish into a new piece that carries the memories of the original along with the new experiences that you've gained."

Amanda tilted her head to the side. "A rebirth. Hmmm. That's a great idea."

"Good." Savannah stepped back. "Now, get yourself enough glass to fill in the gaps and we'll put it in tonight's firing. You'll be able to show Dale the results in class tomorrow morning."

"That's awesome! I've wanted to try one of the new dichromatic samples. Can I use a strip to fill in one of the gaps?"

"Absolutely. Do it." Savannah smiled because she knew the newly arrived, shiny metallic-coated glass would be a magnet for Amanda.

This was exactly the kind of teaching moment that kept her heart singing. Now she understood why her father had been so concerned with continuing to teach beginning glass students. He could have generated far more income with his private commissions, but this feeling was worth more than a few thousand bucks in the bank.

"Oh, before I forget, the next posse meeting is at four in my office. We need to think about our next steps. Can you let Jacob know? I've already told Edward."

Returning to the office, Savannah stood in front of the whiteboard with her hands on her hips. *What are we missing?* She stood there a few moments more and then picked up one of the markers. She added a Vincent O'Neil entry then wrote "Living at The Pier Hotel—no alibi" in the Investigation column with her name assigned.

Checking her watch, she saw it was a little before four. She scrunched her forehead. *Where's Edward? He usually gets here early—with a scrumptious snack.*

"I've got the kiln ready for you to check." Amanda flounced down into the desk chair. Jacob followed, pulling one of the stools in from the classroom. He placed it to the side of the whiteboard and perched on it. Suzy circled twice around the stool and curled up underneath it for a nap.

She checked her watch again and then heard the bell tinkle in the display and retail room. "I'm here!" Edward bellowed. "I've even brought some of our new apricot goodies." He brought a tray into the office stacked with fragrant hot muffins wrapped in triangle papers that had the word *apricot* imprinted along the borders.

He placed the tray on the corner of the desk and sat down in the side chair. Grabbing one of the muffins, he looked up at Savannah. "So, where are we?"

"Nowhere, I'm afraid. So I thought the best way to figure out our next moves would be to review what we all know." Picking up a marker, she pointed to the first suspect on the murder whiteboard. "Frank Lattimer definitely had a loud argument with Megan late on Saturday, but no one knows what it was about, so that line is still active."

Amanda stood and took a blue marker from the shelf. "I identified Vincent as one of Megan's glass team but you're still assigned."

"This next one is mine." Edward leaned forward in the side chair and brushed the muffin crumbs from the front of his shirt. "I've met with Wanda—alone. Which I believe counts for way above the call of duty, but I haven't gotten to the bottom of their conversation. She is avoiding saying anything against Megan. On the other hand, she is as open as a church to gossip about anyone else."

Savannah nodded her head. "Also, we saw her with Vincent not far from the Chihuly Museum. So basically, I think it's time I tackle her alone and try to get an alibi out of her."

Jacob stooped to pick up Suzy. "I'm still looking at the applications. I've sorted them in the obvious ways, but nothing else has come out of that. I'm going to start sorting in obscure orders now."

Savannah looked at the others look at Jacob in amazement. *Only Jacob could call his first approaches obvious.*

"I've been talking to Keith about the intern students, Megan, and her family. He also knows the inside workings of art festivals, which makes him a valuable resource. In fact, I've asked him to our next meeting."

"Hey! Don't we get a vote?" Edward folded his arms and lifted one brow.

Amanda and Jacob looked at Savannah and back at Edward as if they were watching a tennis match.

"Vote?" Savannah crossed her arms. "Megan's death is the issue here. Did you forget?"

"No, of course not." Edward stood and grasped her arms above the elbows. "It's just that we're all involved and you should include us."

Savannah dropped her head on her chest. "You're absolutely right. I should have checked with you first."

"Damn right!" Edward sat and crossed his long slim legs. He grabbed another muffin.

"Okay, I'll start over. Keith is a resource into the lives of Megan, Vincent, and Leon. Does anyone object to adding him to our investigation?"

"Not me." Amanda's eyes switched from Savannah to Edward and back. "I think he's ever so handsome and smart. We need every bit of help we can charm"—she looked at Edward—"into solving this murder." Looking back at Savannah, she continued, "Right, Jacob?"

Jacob held Suzy up to kiss the top of her head right on the tip of her white stripe, then smiled in agreement.

"Okay, we're agreed." Savannah looked back to the whiteboard. "Next suspect is Leon. Edward that one was yours."

"No progress yet. I'll keep working on it."

"The next one is the shards." Savannah scrunched her left eye. "I haven't gotten much further on this one, but Keith says it's a proprietary formula, which could be a major factor in her death. I'll keep that one going."

"What the deal with this one? Relatives." Edward leaned forward in his chair. "I don't remember where we are on that from the last time."

"This one is for Keith to work." She looked at the row. "We need more information about Megan's family and her background. Even Jacob hasn't been able to get further on this through the application data."

Leaning back, Edward said, "Good. He's from Seattle and has the best chance of getting useful information from the family."

"Let me give him a call before I forget." Savannah dialed Keith's cell and he picked up right away. "Hi, Keith, I'm putting you on speaker." She pressed the button and placed the phone on the desk. "I'm with Jacob, Amanda, and Edward. I told them you are willing to question Megan's family in case there are any leads. Is this good for you?"

"Absolutely, I know them slightly. But I'll be the only familiar face here in St. Petersburg. What should I ask?"

"Frankly, we need to make sure that her family has alibis for Saturday after midnight. Also, if they knew of any problems that Megan had, that would be great." Savannah looked at the others and they were nodding in agreement.

"No problem at all."

"Thanks, Keith. I would like for you to come to our next meeting, which will be tomorrow morning at nine in my office."

"I'd be delighted!"

"Thanks again. Bye." She pushed the END CALL button.

"He's going to help a lot," said Amanda.

"What about Vincent?" Savannah asked. "Although Amanda identified Megan's glass team earlier and we tracked down Vincent from Jacob's research, we really don't know much about him."

"Oh, oh, oh." Amanda waved her arm. "Let me do that one. I don't have any assignments."

"No, I think I'll keep this one." Savannah said. "I want you to keep the class on track."

"But—"

Looking into Amanda's crestfallen face, she replied, "Don't worry, I'm reassigning the Frank suspect line to you." She erased her own name and wrote Amanda's in the Assigned To column for Frank Lattimer. "You're the best in social media and we really need to nail down his whereabouts. I'd like to do this as quickly as we can.

"We're doing great guys." Savannah stepped back from the updated whiteboard. "Except that this is taking too long."

"Thanks for the prod." Amanda leaned over and grabbed the last muffin and held it in the air. "Does anyone else want the last muffin?" Seeing all the heads shaking no, she took a bite. "These are irresistible," she mumbled through the crumbs.

"Okay, posse." They all looked at Savannah. She smiled wide. "Let's do our stuff and we'll meet here tomorrow morning with news and progress, I hope."

Edward stood and collected the tray. "Posse? Like in a Wild West movie?"

"Yes."

Standing tall, he replied, "Well, pilgrim, looks like we've got some wrangling to do. I'll see you tomorrow." He tipped two fingers to his imaginary hat and headed for the front door exaggerating a John Wayne swagger.

Savannah giggled. "That's bad, really bad."

Chapter 22

After getting home late after helping Amanda prepare Webb's Glass Shop for the last day of class, Savannah struggled to feed Rooney, take him for a quick calm-down run, and bustle him into her car for his agility training class.

Rooney knew it was class day and took every opportunity to play with his food, tangle himself in his leash, and balk at getting into the car.

"Come on, Rooney," she muttered as she pushed his large hindquarters onto the passenger seat of the car and buckled the restraint clip onto his halter. "You love this class and you love the instructor. Why do you always make things difficult?"

Rooney was the essence of puppy innocence when he looked at her on their way to the training facility. It was a longish drive to the training grounds, but it was the best training facility in the state. This would be Rooney's last chance to brush up before his first competitive trial on Saturday.

The training session began ordinarily enough with puppy and parent stretches before running a few laps around the practice yard.

"Hi, Linda," Savannah said, waving a hand to a stocky woman with tanned wrinkles around smiling eyes and a perpetually positive attitude.

"Hey, Savannah," said the instructor. "Are you ready to put Rooney through his paces?"

"If you think he's ready."

Linda knelt on one knee and took Rooney's large head into her hands. "Oh yes, he's ready." She looked into his eyes. "He looks bright and fit. It should be fun for him."

"As you suspected, he needed to do something very focused after my dad died. He's been wonderful since we started these classes."

"Good." Linda stood up. "This is his second month of beginner classes, isn't it? He's already accomplished weave-pole training and contact obstacle performance. This class reviews on jumps, tunnels, and chutes and will finish his schooling in the basics."

"That's great to hear," said Savannah.

Linda ran her hands down Rooney's back and felt his shoulders and haunches. "After formal class is over, I'd like to run him through the course a few times for a little extra tuning."

Savannah looked over at the structures built into a small enclosure. "He loves the course I made in the backyard, but it's nowhere near the size of this one."

Linda smiled. "That's good that he has constant reinforcement at home. He has lots of potential."

The routine training started with the class of eight dogs and eight owners running laps around the practice field. The first laps began with the dogs on leash; then Linda instructed them to begin running off leash. As usual, there was a bit of a rodeo with some dogs running to play with their classmates and owners shouting, pleading, and commanding obedience.

Savannah proudly stood by the attentive Rooney, who stood tall but relaxed beside her. *He is such a good dog. I wonder if he still remembers Dad. It's been several months, but I'm so grateful for his company. He has recovered beautifully.*

Linda stood by the gate that led to the enclosed agility course. "Today we're going to practice the final obstacle, the tunnel. For some dogs, this is where they wash out. Your dog has to trust that this tunnel is safe for him to dash through even when he can't see the end. Your job is to send your dog into the entrance, then coax him from the exit."

"What if he gets stuck?" piped up the very large owner of a papillon terrier.

"We'll see some of that today," said Linda. "I have several ways to coax a reluctant pet through the tunnel. Worst case, we crawl in there and lead them out."

"Yuk, that's not good."

"So, line up from smallest dog to largest. We'll start by leading your dog to the entrance of the tunnel. At the entrance, you command him to sit and stay; then you go to the other end of the tunnel and command him to come. Okay? Let's try it."

The smallest dog with the largest owner attempted the instructions. The little white papillon, however, just couldn't stay behind while her owner went to the other end of the tunnel. She kept trotting along behind him like a little white tufted caboose.

"Okay, let me hold her while you get to the other end," Linda offered and scooped up the little terrier. When the owner made it to the end of the tunnel, Linda let the terrier see her owner through the tunnel, but held fast. "Now call her."

When the owner said, "Come," the little dickens shot through the tunnel like lightning and leapt up onto her owner's chest licking his face like it was covered with cherry pie. Everyone laughed.

The class progressed through the remaining dogs until the only pair left was Rooney and Savannah. She led him up to the entrance of the tunnel and commanded him to sit and stay. When she walked to the other end of the tunnel, Rooney trotted along behind her very much like the little terrier had earlier.

Patiently, Savannah led him by pulling on his collar back to the tunnel entrance and repeated her command to sit and stay. Once again, he sat until she was at the other end and then he followed her before she could call him.

"Savannah, does he have trust issues?" Linda put her hands on her hips and frowned at Rooney.

"Possibly." Savannah led Rooney back to the tunnel entrance and Linda stood next to Rooney. "He was completely devoted to my dad, and when he died I think Rooney felt abandoned."

"Okay, let me give you and Rooney a little after class instruction so as not to hold up everyone." Savannah was relieved to be out of the spotlight and she and Rooney waited at the sidelines until the rest of the dogs and their owners had gone.

After everyone had left, Linda motioned for them to return to the tube. "Thanks for waiting. Let's try the same trick." Linda stooped in front of the entrance with her hand holding Rooney's collar. As soon as Savannah was out of sight, Rooney tried to follow. "Stay, Rooney." He tried again with calm persistence, dragging the sturdy Linda along.

"Rooney!" Savannah scurried back and sat on the ground in front of him. He practically covered her face with licks and sat in her lap. She looked at Linda. "Any other ideas? We're entered in the puppy agility competition the day after tomorrow. Do you think I should withdraw?"

"Let me think a minute." Linda struggled up and stood scratching the back of her neck.

She looked at Savannah's tall, slim frame. "Do you think you can crawl through the tunnel?"

"Sure, it's pretty big." Savannah leaned over and peered through the tunnel. "Yeah, I can do this."

"Good, I want you to crawl through backward so that Rooney can follow and assure him that there's nothing bad in there."

"That might work." Savannah backed into the bright yellow hose and crept backward calling as she went, "Rooney, come on, Rooney boy." He dropped down to his haunches and scooted Lassie style through the tunnel. "Good boy, good boy" was all that was heard from the tunnel.

The first thing that appeared from the tunnel was Savannah's feet and then her butt as she scuffled out. As soon as she cleared it, Rooney ran through the tunnel, jumped into her lap, and tumbled her onto her back. "So, now you're happy. You're pretty smart." Savannah scratched him behind the ears with both hands.

"Okay, let's try again." Linda walked around to the front of the tunnel. "Bring him around for a second trial."

Savannah called for Rooney and led him to the front of the tunnel. He looked down at the opening and then up at Savannah in a sorrowful tilt. "He's acting as if I'm going to send him to Siberia."

"It could be that that is exactly what he's thinking. Anyway, try it again."

Savannah signaled for Rooney to sit. He folded his rump under himself in the slowest possible way. Savannah then pointed to the entrance of the tunnel and said, "Go, Rooney!" as she ran around to the exit. Rooney got up on all four legs, made a yipping circle, and followed her to the end of the tunnel then just stared at her. "This is frustrating."

"Now don't give up. We have lots of tricks up our sleeve. Let's try an advanced technique." Moving to the entrance of the tunnel, Linda said, "I want you to start at the beginning of the course and run the whole thing with Rooney just as we've trained. In the heat of the run, he might do this one as well. He is very eager to please."

"That's very true." Savannah sounded doubtful. "I'll try anything you say."

"Now when you get to the tunnel, you'll already be running, so point to the tunnel and run around to the end and see if he gets the idea. I'll stand interference by the entrance. He's a smart puppy and should be fine."

Nodding agreement, Savannah jogged over to the start of the course and Rooney obediently trotted beside her. The start and finish were on top of a small wooden platform. She commanded Rooney to stay at the starting line and she crouched ready to run.

Linda pulled a red bandana out of her pocket and waved them a start signal.

Savannah yelled, "Go, Rooney!" and ran for the first obstacle, which was a simple hurdle over a plastic bar, and Rooney cleared it easily. A tire suspended at four points on a white pipe structure followed that and Rooney jumped through with ease. The next was a set of parallel poles in a straight line called a weave for him to run in and out. It looked like his body was making an "s," he sped through it so quickly.

The next to last training obstacle was the tunnel. As Rooney left the weave, Linda and Savannah both pointed to the entrance and Rooney bolted through it without the least hesitation and at Savannah's direction skittered across the seesaw, then hopped onto the platform for a stunning finish.

"Wow! That was an incredible run." Linda ran over to the platform and gave Rooney a hearty slap on the rump. "If you do that on Saturday, you're going to waltz out of there with a first-place prize."

"I'm hoping for a safe and nonmortifying run," said Savannah. "Right, Rooney?"

Rooney tilted his head to the side and looked adorable.

Chapter 23

Friday Morning

As soon as she settled Rooney for the day, Savannah grabbed her backpack and headed over to McCloud's and parked in the empty visitor's parking lot. She walked around the outside of the gallery and back to the hot shop.

As she expected, each of the hot glass stations was occupied and Duncan McCloud was overseeing the operation off to the side. He turned as she walked up.

"Hi, Savannah, this is an early call. What's up?"

"Good morning, Duncan. I need your expert opinion on a small bit of glass. Do you have a few moments?"

"Sure, what do you need?"

"It really needs to be on a light table to see properly. Can we look at the glass now or do I need to wait until your students are done?"

Duncan looked at the operations and nodded

to Savannah. "This beginner team is almost finished and then it will be twenty minutes until I need to monitor their next piece."

Savannah smiled her thanks and perched on the observation bleachers to wait. The beginner team only needed help with the final scoring to make sure it was deep enough for the small vase to crack off the blow pipe.

Duncan congratulated the team and made sure that they had it safely stored in the annealing kiln. "Okay, Savannah. Let's look at your glass."

They went inside the gallery building into a small preparation workshop, and Duncan pressed the ON switch to a large table. The light shone through an opaque glass top with a soft glow. Savannah pulled the envelope out of her backpack and spilled the shards out onto the surface of the light table. "Can you tell me how this glass was made and what makes it so luminous?"

Duncan bent over the crimson shards and then lifted a pair of strong magnifiers from the pegboard wall and pulled them over his head. After adjusting the fit, he said, "I've seen this before. It is part of what Megan was working so hard to perfect."

"I don't understand?"

"One of the glass suppliers has formulated a new copper ruby especially suited to the typical soda lime batches that we use here in the studio. Unlike other colors based on gold, silver, or, for that matter, cadmium selenium glasses, which do not substantially change, copper ruby requires particular care during the curing or it turns dark and dull or, even worse, clear."

"But if it's readily available, why was her technique so valuable?"

"If she had discovered a sure-fire process, she could have made a fortune selling beautiful figures as well as enjoying an open-armed welcome at any hot glass shop in the world teaching that process."

Getting to Webb's Glass Shop a little before nine, Savannah unlocked the back door and dropped her backpack on the floor beside the oak rolltop desk and dropped the keys on its worn surface. She went through the classroom and into the display and retail room, unlocked the front door, and pressed the START button on the register. It slowly booted after the hard drive whirred and groaned, then displayed the startup screen and settled into a satisfied hum.

I'm really going to have to get a better machine.

The front-door bell jangled and Amanda appeared in a cotton candy froth of pink and violet carrying three large flat boxes of Krispy Kreme donuts. Her feet were clad in closed-toe Wellington rain boots in pink with violet polka dots.

Savannah held the door while Amanda struggled to set the boxes down on the checkout counter. "I've brought a treat for the class. This is graduation day!"

"Indeed it is."

"I also brought one box just for the posse. I'm

sure we deserve it, and we need to make sure that Edward gets a taste of a southern treat. I called him when I was at the drive-thru so he wouldn't bake anything."

The door bell jangled once more as Jacob stepped into the shop carrying Suzy in his arms. He wrinkled his nose. "What's that smell?"

"Krispy Kreme donuts." Amanda lifted the lid of the top box and the smell of warm glazed sugar exploded into the room. "Edward has never tasted them."

One more door bell jangle announced Edward's arrival. He was carrying a large carafe of coffee with four mugs. "Wow, those smell good. Are they the donuts you were telling me about?"

"Yes." Amanda waved a Vanna White wave over the donuts. "I got the two most popular types, the warm glazed and the custard-filled chocolate. Try one of each so we know which team you're on."

Jacob placed Suzy on the floor, then reached into the box for one of the shiny circles. "I'm glazed. That's my favorite."

Amanda snagged one of the chocolate custards. "I'm filled."

Edward looked at Savannah with his eyebrows raised. Savannah smiled. "I'm not going to tell you. This is an important choice you need to make on your own."

"Okay." Edward picked up one in each hand. He tasted the glazed. "Mmm. That's awesome. What a perfect combination of sweet dough and sugar." He tasted the filled. "That's perfect as well. The custard is the right texture and the dough is light and sweet. They're both brilliant."

Savannah smiled. "Right, but which one is your favorite?"

"Both."

Jacob reached for another glazed. "You can't have two favorites. That makes no sense."

"Okay, okay." Edward took another bite of the filled donut. "Definitely the crème filled. It reminds me of the custard we serve over bread pudding. I love them." He looked at Savannah. "Which one are you?"

"I'm a traditionalist." She reached into the box. "It's glazed for me." She took a huge bite out of one of the glazed donuts. "However, to experience the full impact, you need to go to the store and have them pick out one right off the manufacturing line." She chomped another enormous bite with a mischievous grin, then popped the remaining bit into her mouth and licked her fingers. "Those are out of this world."

"I'll have to try that." Edward finished his crème donut.

"Let's take the coffee back to the office and make our update there."

They settled into their self-assigned stools and chairs. Edward served coffee all around and Suzy curled herself up for a nap in the dog basket by the back door.

This is becoming a comfortable routine for us. Is this a good thing?

Savannah settled into the oak rolling office chair

and cupped her coffee with both hands. "Let's review. First, Amanda. What's up with Frank?"

"Well, I'm lucky that he's so well connected socially in the community. He's on Facebook, Twitter, and Pinterest all the time. I verified that right after his argument with Megan, Frank gave a speech at the monthly meeting at The Bob Graham Center for Public Service. His presentation was about the effect of the Buy Local movement in small cities."

"But the argument was on Friday. When was the speech?"

"It was on Saturday morning. The University of Florida sponsored the series of presentations and it's about a three-hour drive north of Tampa. He spent the weekend with faculty friends, and there's a Facebook check-in late on Friday night at The Fat Tuscan Café. Then he arrived at his shop late on Monday. His alibis are watertight with so many people confirming what social media already says."

"But can't you preprogram your posts for Facebook?"

"Sure, if it's your account. You can prearrange the post times of everything for several days."

"So that's no proof then?" Savannah grabbed a marker and walked up to their whiteboard.

"Hang on there. I said you could post in advance. You can't participate in shared posts with multiple group photos in advance. It's all documented as it occurs in real time." The other three stared at Amanda. She put her hands on her ample hips. "That means he couldn't have done it. He was liking, commenting, and generating posts until the wee hours of Saturday morning. Well after the time of Megan's death."

Edward took the pen from Savannah's hand. "That means that Frank is in the clear." He drew a single line through all the words in the entire first row, put the pen back in her hand, and sat back down in his chair.

"Grrrrr, that's hugely disappointing." Savannah took the pen and added another line through each of the words. "I really wanted it to be Frank." She sighed deeply. "It would make my life so much easier." She slumped back into the oak chair, awakening an alarming squeak from its vintage spring.

Amanda grabbed the pen from Savannah and crossed out all the words in the second line. "I've already identified Megan's team. I don't think this is a lead anymore." Savannah turned, then pointed to Edward. "That leaves Wanda Quitman as still an active line of inquiry."

"Yeah, I need some ideas. She doesn't seem the murdering type."

Savannah tilted her head. "No one on our list seems to be a murderer." She sipped her coffee and placed the cup on the work surface of the rolltop desk. "But she does keep popping up everywhere we turn."

"There's got to be a way to confirm an alibi." Edward stood and walked up to the whiteboard. "Maybe we're overthinking this. With everything she does for all these organizations, she's got to have an assistant. Right?"

Amanda frowned as she lifted the lid of the Krispy Kreme box. "Then why haven't we met the assistant?" She picked out a custard-filled donut.

"Good question. Wanda's in the public too much to do all the administration by herself, but I think she wants everyone to believe how busy she is. Maybe she's keeping the assistant a secret." Savannah rubbed her hands together. "That's your next task, Edward." She added "Find assistant" to Wanda's Investigation column on the whiteboard.

"Oh joy, more time in Wanda land." Edward folded his arms.

"I'm still looking at the application records." Jacob looked directly at his name on the murder whiteboard. "There is something more there. I know it. I just know it. But it's not yet clear. I need more time." He scooped up Suzy and left the office to head back into the custom workshop and his piles of sorted applications.

The remaining posse watched him go.

Stepping back, Savannah looked down the rows. "Next is Leon and that one is assigned to Edward, but I think"—she looked back to Amanda—"you should tackle that one now that you've cleared Frank. Is that okay with you?"

"Yep."

Savannah sat back in the oak chair. "I have an update on the glass shards. I showed them to Duncan McCloud early this morning and he recognized the glass that Megan used. It is not only a special glass but the processes used to anneal or cool the glass are what makes that color so beautiful. Megan had the knack for the process and was keeping it her secret. There would have been no hint during the making of her pieces. The secret technique was afterward, when she could cool the pieces in privacy."

"How does that help?" Amanda asked.

Savannah marked through that row. "It doesn't help. Megan would need to be alive for that process to be shared." She sighed and plopped down again.

Edward poured more of the coffee into his mug. "How's Keith doing with Megan's relatives?"

"I haven't heard from him." She frowned. "That doesn't sound right. I'll give him a call and remind him. I thought I had invited him to this meeting. Do you remember if I did?"

Edward took another filled donut. "You most certainly did. I most definitely heard you. Definitely." He took a large bite.

"Maybe he's meeting with the family now," Amanda shot back at Edward. "We should give him a chance. None of us are professionals."

"That's worrying. I was counting on him." Savannah wrote "call" under Keith's name. "I'm sure things are progressing, but I'll check."

She stepped back to look at the whiteboard. "So, the only remaining row is mine for Vincent."

"What are you going to do?" asked Edward.

"I'm going to try to reach him through his art. I'll ask him to come here to the shop and maybe we can all help him feel more comfortable with us."

"Why would he come here?"

"I'm going to suggest that he teach a private class to me and Amanda."

Stepping up to the whiteboard, Savannah wrote "Verify alibi" in the Investigation column and her own name in the Assigned To column.

Amanda clapped her hands together. "That's great. We can make him comfortable and get something out of him."

"What's his forte?" said Edward.

"It's embarrassing that I don't know. That's one more thing that I need to ask Keith."

They were interrupted by the front-door bell jangling followed by Keith calling out, "Savannah?"

She leaned into the open doorway. "We're back here. Thanks for coming."

"Sorry I'm late. I banged my knee in the shower and there was more traffic than I thought down Central Avenue." Keith looked at the gathering and limped back into the classroom to grab a work stool, then placed it beside Edward facing the whiteboard.

Edward grabbed a cup from Savannah's desk, checked to make sure it was clean, then poured Keith a cup of coffee. "This will calm your nerves. Driving in St. Pete is an adventure in avoidance."

"No problem, we were getting to your row." Savannah smiled and erased the "call" reminder next to Keith's name.

"I don't have particularly good news for you. It was very easy to verify that Megan's family was all in Seattle over the weekend—both parents and the sister. So . . ." He took the marker from

Savannah and crossed out the Relatives row. He gave it back to Savannah.

Savannah looked at the whiteboard. "Ugh, I'm getting depressed with our progress. Lack of progress is more accurate."

Edward stood and took the tray. "No one said this was going to be easy. I think it's going to get harder."

Savannah placed her cup on the tray. "I agree. I still can't imagine that Megan needed to die for any reason. Anyway, let's meet at Queen's Head tonight to touch bases. Six o'clock. Good?"

Edward, Keith, and Amanda nodded while still looking at the whiteboard.

They heard the front-door bell clash its loudest. "That would be the Rosenberg twins." Amanda put her cup on Edward's tray. "I told them about the Krispy Kreme donuts so they're here extra early." She raised her eyebrows, smiled wide, and plunged through the door into the classroom.

Edward looked into Savannah's eyes. "You know, it's okay if you want to stop this. Detective Parker is perfectly capable of solving Megan's murder without your help."

"He's perfectly capable, but I want to solve this case and bring justice to Megan. She died too young. The world will be much poorer because we lost all the art she could have shared."

Chapter 24

The twins were wearing orange today. Savannah felt like putting on her sunglasses to protect her eyes. Where on earth did they find those Capri slacks? Nope, she didn't want to know. Ignorance in this case was indeed bliss.

"Good morning, Faith. Good morning, Rachel."

"It's a cool morning for May." Faith led them back to the classroom. "I'm happy this is our last day."

Rachel grumbled, "I'm happy we have Krispy Kreme donuts to look forward to. I don't want this class to end."

"Thanks, ladies. That's nice. Go on back to the office. Amanda has set up a little table for the donuts and coffee. Enjoy."

As they made their way, Savannah followed them. She snagged another glazed donut. "You know, I've been thinking about establishing an open studio for experienced students. Is that something you would be interested in?"

The twins looked at each other. Faith smiled and turned to Savannah. "How will that work?"

"I'm thinking of setting up two more workstations in the custom workshop so you could work on projects of your choosing. You could sign up for a month at a time."

Rachel piped up, "That might fit us exactly, but would we be able to get instruction?"

"Not the same type of dedicated class instruction that you get with a workshop, but certainly we'd all be around for consultation and advice. What do you think?"

The twins looked at each other again. "That's a great idea," said Faith.

"But we need to think about it." Rachel eyed a "keep this to ourselves" look at Faith.

"We need to discuss this at home," said Faith.

"Fair enough." Savannah helped herself to another donut. "I'll get things set up and give you first refusal in about a week. Sound good?"

"That sounds like a great idea," said Dale.

They all looked at Dale, who had quietly entered and was placing his materials on his workbench. He leaned in to look into the office. "If you two don't take up the offer, I certainly will."

Amanda raised her eyebrows and gently bit her lip.

Savannah nodded. "Okay, I'll see if I can get three spaces fitted out."

Dale walked over to Amanda. "I'm so sorry

that I broke your platter yesterday. I can make you another one if you'll help me."

"No need for that. Savannah and I made a completely new one from the shards of the original. We'll see it this morning when we unload the kiln. It should be gorgeous."

"Oh, that's nice."

Amanda pointed to the donut box on the small folding table. "It's the last day of the workshop—help yourself."

Dale smiled broadly at Amanda. "Delighted. My favorite is the custard-filled one."

"That's mine, too!"

Holding the chocolate-covered donut in his hand, Dale turned to Savannah and asked, "About how much would this open studio cost?"

"I'm thinking a hundred dollars a month. That's about the same price as a workshop and I'd throw in a fifteen percent discount on supplies."

The Canadian students filed in, followed by Helen. The donuts were a big hit and they disappeared in a flash.

"Now that we've had our treat"—Savannah removed the two empty boxes leaving the third box in the office and put them in the recycle bin—"it's time for our last lesson." She led the way back into the classroom.

After everyone had chatted and then settled she continued, "Our last topic is called coldworking. That means whatever you do to your glass piece after it comes out of the kiln. First, we need to see what our work looks like after being fired. Amanda, let's take them over to the kiln."

The class trooped into the custom workshop and gathered around the large kiln. Savannah waited until everyone settled down and had a good view of the front of the kiln. "This is what it looks like after the full cycle has been processed. The panel on the front flashes CMPLT along with the internal temperature. Once the temperature is under a hundred degrees, that means it's safe to open the kiln to outside air."

"This is quite heavy, so stand back." With both hands, Savannah grabbed the long metal handle that ran the length of the front of the kiln and lifted it open with a grunt. Standing to the side, she said, "Now, you can see what Amanda and I look at every morning."

The class peered down into the kiln.

"That doesn't look at all like what I expected." Nancy leaned over to look down into the kiln. "What a dusty mess."

Amanda laughed. "Goodness, that's what I said the first time Savannah showed it to me."

"Yuk, so we have to wash this off every time?" Miss Carter wrinkled her nose.

"Right on target. This happens every morning after a fuse. I'm going to hand each of you your fired piece so you can take it over to the sink and rinse off the ash. You know the drill from Tuesday's lesson. Amanda and I will clean the slumping molds later."

Amanda sighed dramatically. "My pleasure, your majesty."

"There's another rinsing sink back in the office, so split up and get them clean and dry. Then take them to your worktables so we can evaluate our final steps."

Each member of the class took a turn rinsing off the dust and ash from their fused pieces. They also made a huge dent in the stacks of old T-shirts to be used for drying them. Everyone finally made their way back to the classroom with a shiny new dish in front of them.

Savannah looked over the class. "Today, we'll learn how to improve your glassworks by cold-working them. Coldworking is any process that changes glass in its room temperature state. This includes sandblasting, grinding, sanding, drilling, cutting, engraving, or polishing the glass. Usually this is done during the finishing stages of your glass fusing. Now, let's see who needs to do what."

Working her way around the room, she held up each student's glass piece and determined what the final finishing steps would be. Dale's needed a bit of sanding on one edge while Helen's needed some grinding to square up the edges. The Canadians didn't need any cold-working at all, and the twins were arguing over the need for more work or could they count the imperfections as "artistic" effects.

She was in the middle of her "make it as good as you can make it" lecture to the twins when the front-door bell jangled. "Amanda, take over, please."

In the display and retail room was Officer

Boulli, tapping his foot with his arms folded across his generous, round belly. "Hey, I've got some more questions for you. Is here okay or do you want to go downtown?"

"You're bluffing." She walked up and stood in front of him with her arms folded. "Detective Parker doesn't work that way."

Crestfallen, Officer Boulli gulped and pulled a small brown paper bag from his back pocket. It had a printed label with bold red lettering proclaiming EVIDENCE as well as dates and signatures.

Savannah raised her eyebrows and relaxed her arms and shoulders.

"This is some glass evidence that the pathologist found in the victim. Detective Parker thought you might be able to help identify them." He handed over the small packet.

"Why didn't he give these to Frank Lattimer?"

Officer Boulli raised his shoulders up and down and replied, "He did."

"So you're checking Frank's answers against mine." She folded her arms across her chest. "That's having your cake and eating it too."

He nodded and let slip a sly little grin.

Savannah walked over to the light box by the glass shelves and turned it on. She opened the little brown bag and jiggled the tiny glass shards onto the surface. They were the same type of glass that she and Edward had collected at the park.

She looked up and found Officer Boulli wandering around looking at various student works that were offered for sale. "Are you waiting for an answer?"

He picked up one of the larger platters, making Savannah cringe. "Yep, I can't let them out of my sight."

So much for that. He hadn't looked at them once since he handed over the bag. She put on her over-the-head magnifiers and confirmed that this was the same type of glass that she and Edward had found. Slipping off the glasses, she stood over the tiny shards.

Where did you come from? Did Megan make these locally?

"I'd like to call in another expert. Can you stay?"

"I don't know." He stood looking at her.

She lowered her head to give him her schoolteacher look. "Well, can you call Detective Parker and find out?"

He sighed deeply and pulled out his cell phone. "Wait until I check." He turned his back to her and looked out at the street.

Savannah shook her head slowly. *He's not doing anything wrong, but it sure seems like it.*

Amanda leaned through the classroom door. "Can you break away for a second? Helen has a question I can't answer."

"Sure." She looked back at Officer Boulli, who, from the tapping of his toe, was apparently on hold.

Helen pounced as soon as Savannah walked through the door. "I'm not happy with this at all. I can't really see a difference in the side that

I've been grinding versus the side that is still untouched. What is wrong?"

Picking up the little dish, Savannah ran her fingers over the edges and could feel that one side had been ground, but only very finely. "I think you might be using the wrong grit. Which grinder are you using?"

Helen pointed to the smaller of the two grinders in the back of the classroom.

"Ah, that's the one with a fine grit. That's mostly for polishing and small imperfections. Try the bigger one and see what happens."

Amanda mouthed *Thank you* from across the room as Helen calmed down and began to square up her dish using the right equipment.

Officer Boulli filled the doorway and blocked the afternoon sunlight. "Detective Parker says I can stay here another hour if it helps the investigation."

Savannah moved deliberately toward the doorway and Officer Boulli stumbled over his feet getting out of the way. "I'll see if Duncan, owner of the Duncan McCloud Gallery, can come over to look at this."

She used the phone by the cash register and in a very few words sealed the deal. "He's coming right over. He's only five minutes away."

Biting the inside of her cheek to keep a straight face, she said, "Today is the last day of our workshop so we have donuts. They're in the office if you'd like one."

Boulli's eyes widened and he immediately walked into the office and snagged one. Through his munching, he asked, "Have you got an extra cup for coffee?"

"Sure." Savannah pulled a spare cup from the bottom drawer of her desk. As she handed it over to Boulli, she noted that there were only two of the six donuts left. "There's no milk left, but you're welcome to the sugar." About fifteen minutes later, Savannah was pleased to see McCloud nearly shake the door bell off its hook as he plunged into the display and retail room. "Hey! Is this real? Am I really going to help in a murder investigation?"

"Yes you are. I need some help identifying a few shards of glass. They're here on the light table." She handed him the over-the-head magnifiers.

He put them on and selected one of the tweezers that were on the light table and used them to move the shards around. "Oh, this is such beautiful glass. This is exactly like the shards you showed me on Wednesday. I've done my research and I remember seeing something like this in Italy when I was a student there."

"When was that?"

He looked up and removed the magnifiers. "That was way back in the seventies. This was a new process that held great promise for easy to create reds—but it was abandoned."

"Why?"

"It had two major problems. It was very expensive to create because it required so much copper."

"And the second reason?"

"It was incredibly toxic. The inventor inhaled deadly fumes and died a painful, horrible death."

"Why didn't he wear a mask?" Officer Boulli asked.

"They didn't know." Savannah shuddered at the thought of an artist poisoned by his medium and was frustrated by Boulli's complete lack of knowledge about the birthplace of glassmaking.

Chapter 25

The funky décor in the Queen's Head Pub always provoked Savannah to smile at the dry, British tongue-in-cheek humor. The walls were a modern slate color and supported multiple plaster-cast architectural shelves mounted near the ceiling. They were painted white and overflowing with British symbolic icons: a head of the queen statue, a porcelain bulldog, milk glass vases filled with white plastic flowers, and tons of books. It was hard to explain but a pleasure to experience.

Keith, Amanda, Edward, and Jacob had chosen a table outside at the far end of the patio. It was the one area avoided by regular customers until all other seating had been claimed. Suzy was lying under Jacob's chair and raised her head as Savannah led Rooncy to the table.

"Hi, guys. I thought it was about time for Suzy and Rooney to meet."

"Yes, Miss Savannah." Jacob led Suzy around the table. The size difference was enormous, but Suzy took charge immediately and let Rooney know she was the lead dog. Rooney stood still for the introductory sniffing, then lay flat on the ground to keep his head lower than Suzy's.

"Wow," said Amanda, "I thought that might have gone the other way."

"Suzy is a trained working dog," said Jacob. "She has responsibilities. Her job is to warn me if I'm having an anxiety attack."

After the dogs settled the dominance chain, Suzy went back under Jacob's chair and Rooney barely squeezed under Savannah's chair. He at least rested his head on his paws. His wagging tail was a definite trip hazard, so she pulled him out and had him lay under the table.

Finally, Savannah looked up as the waitress was standing over her with a patient smile.

"Nicole, it's great to see you back." Savannah stood and gave her a hug. "How are your niece and nephew in Switzerland?"

"They are rock stars. They're seven and nine now and such great fun." Nicole smiled with loving eyes bright and gooey. "We all went to Disneyland Paris. My brother-in-law is delightfully rich so I wallowed in luxury the whole time."

"Family is good; rich family is even better." Savannah sat and looked down at Rooney, then across at Edward.

"Is that a new tattoo? It's gorgeous," said Amanda, peering at the morning glory vine wrapping its way up Nicole's left arm. "The hummingbird is perfect at the shoulder. It looks like it could fly away any moment."

"Yeah, I found a new guy. He's great. Expensive, because his shop is close to downtown, but he's really talented." Nicole pulled out an order pad. "We've got some crispy chickpeas and artichoke hummus coming. Drinks are on Edward, so what's your poison?"

"I don't want poison. I want a root beer," said Jacob clearly, and he even looked directly at Nicole.

"Got it." Nicole looked at Amanda. "Your regular?" Amanda nodded and Nicole wrote on her pad. Looking at Savannah, she asked, "Beach Blonde Ale?" Savannah nodded. Then to Keith, she prompted, "And you, sir?"

"I'll have the house red."

Nicole made a note, then looked up and said, "Boss?"

Edward leaned back in his chair. "Let me try that new amber ale we got from Brewer's Tap Room. It's been getting good reviews. What's it called?"

"Tropic Thunder."

"Yep, that's it."

Nicole left and Savannah turned in her chair and reached down to help Rooney get more comfortable. As she leaned over, the chair leg scraped, startling Rooney, who bolted up, his toenails desperately scrambling for a quick escape from the angry chair. The chair lost the gravity battle and tipped over with Savannah grabbing air. With a plop, she landed on her scraped leg and let out a screech.

The whole gang gasped, then scrambled, but Edward was the first to reach her. "Are you hurt?"

Keith came around from the other side. "Let me help you up." He grabbed her upper arms and pulled her upright in a jiffy.

"I'm fine," she panted. "Rooney got startled."

Amanda pointed down at Savannah's leg. "Look, you're bleeding."

The fall had broken open the scrape and blood soaked through the gauze as well as her pale blue jeans. "Damn, I'll have to dress it again."

"Again?" Edward's voice lowered an octave. "When did you get this?"

Jacob handed Savannah a stack of napkins he had quietly taken from one of the server's stations. "Thanks." She pressed the stack against her soaked jeans. "I was attacked yesterday morning on our run. I didn't say anything because I didn't want to worry you guys. Edward, do you have a first aid kit?"

"It's in the kitchen. Amanda, help her into the ladies' loo and I'll hand it in to you."

Amanda circled an arm around Savannah's shoulders to hold her up so she could hop through the pub into the ladies' room. Before they could even get the door closed, Edward handed Amanda the first aid kit.

He looked fiercely at Savannah. "We'll be

wanting to know everything in detail. Everything.
In. Detail." He closed the door.

Amanda helped Savannah sit down on the
small stool in the restroom, then rolled up her
jeans and lifted the blood-soaked gauze bandage. "Oh boy, that looks angry." Amanda pulled
away the gauze, rummaged in the first aid kit,
and found a compress. "Now be still so the bleeding will stop." She held the pad on the scrape for
a few minutes, lifted it, and changed pads. "There,
it's stopped."

Savannah fidgeted. "I can finish it."

"Yes, you can, but I'm your friend and I'm
going to do it. I change lots of dressings at my
mother's nursing home. I'm the best you have
right now."

Savannah pressed her lips closed and sat back
and relaxed.

Amanda cleaned the scrape with a wipe and
applied an antiseptic cream. She efficiently
bandaged the wound in gauze and tape. Method-
ically replacing the supplies in the first aid kit,
she said, "This should be good until tomorrow
morning. Do you have enough supplies?"

"Yes, I've got plenty, but, I have to admit, I'm
nowhere as good as you are with bandaging."
She watched as Amanda carefully unrolled the
leg of her jeans back down over the bandage.
"That will give it more protection. It's not a very
good look, but I think you can carry it off."

"I'm not worried about my look. I'm worried
about the look Edward gave me. He was furious."

As they left the ladies' room, Savannah let
Amanda lead to delay even a few more seconds
the reaction she knew was coming from Edward.
She walked to her chair carefully, suppressing
the instinct to favor the newly bandaged leg.

"Precisely when were you going to tell us
about the attack?" Edward spoke so quietly it
sent a nervous ripple down Savannah's spine.
He was using every inch of his British accent to
its fully cultured effect.

"I'm sorry, guys." Savannah looked around
the table. "I didn't want to worry you. That was
a mistake."

"Damn straight it was a mistake." Amanda
frowned. "We're your friends. We've been through
a lot these past few months. We deserve better."

"She's right." Keith looked at Edward. "Family
deserves better."

Savannah pressed her lips tight and lowered
her head. "I agree. I have difficulty with trust.
I apologize."

Jacob pulled Suzy into his lap. "What happened?"
Bless the directness of youth.

"Yesterday morning, I was running with Rooney
along the seawall very near where I discovered
Megan's body. Someone tore out of the trees
and tried to throw me into Tampa Bay."

"Holy moly," Amanda blurted. "Do you think
it was the killer?"

"Can you identify him?" Keith asked.

"I didn't even get a tiny glance at his face.
I thought it was a mugger." She looked over at
Edward, who was sitting straight up, his face

flushed from throat to cheeks. "He was dressed in black with a hoodie pulled low, but I still felt that it was a man."

"How did you know?"

"It was his scent. I recall a musky cologne. I know I've come across it before, but that must be the reason I think it was a man. I really didn't get a sense of height, but definitely strong enough to pitch me off the seawall."

"Why didn't you fall into the water?" Jacob asked.

"My recovery balance is excellent and Rooney was heroic. He launched at the man, bowled him over, and was able to rip off a piece of his pants. I've never heard a more frightening growl. The attacker scrambled up and ran for his life."

Amanda downed the last of her drink. "Did you call nine-one-one?"

"No, I wasn't badly hurt, and I didn't want to be whisked away to an emergency room for such a small scrape." She looked down at her leg.

Amanda looked down at her leg and then back up to stare pointedly.

"Okay, given the trouble I'm having, that's what I should have done. On the other hand, I called Detective Parker, but really had nothing to tell him. He came out himself rather than sending Officer Boulli."

Edward stood and began collecting their empty glasses. "Savannah, this is important. We care about you very much. You are fiercely independent and we love that about you, but it is frustrating when you hide things from us."

"It's hurtful," said Amanda. "It's like you really don't see us as your friends."

Jacob held Suzy tighter. "You should always tell us the truth. We need the truth."

"We need your word of honor that you will be open and unstinting with the full and absolute truth from now on." Edward stood at the end of their table.

"I promise and please forgive me." She felt a warm, cozy flush start from her stomach and settle deep in her chest.

Why am I feeling so good about being chewed out? Oh, it's because they care. That's good.

Savannah looked each of her posse in the eye and said. "I promise, I promise, I promise, I promise" to each of them. Now can we review the case?"

"Nope, not yet." Edward opened the door to the pub. "I'll ask Nicole to get us another round of drinks and then we'll try to figure out how to manage the threat to Savannah."

They each were silent and looked at each other with owl eyes. In a flash, Edward was back and sat down. He placed his elbows on the table and steepled his fingers. "I propose that we take turns protecting Savannah. Who's willing to do what this weekend?"

"I can go to the agility meeting tomorrow morning," Jacob said. "Suzy will be welcome."

"Since that is such a public event, I think we should all be there." Edward looked at Savannah. "What time does it start?"

"We have to sign in at eight. Don't forget about Rooney." Savannah bent down and scratched his blue-gray ears. "He did a good job at the park."

Amanda looked from Edward to Savannah. "What about until the meet starts? Who's going to stay with you tonight?"

"I really don't think—"

Keith interrupted, "Obviously, but we think it's vital."

Savannah's shoulders slumped and she looked down. "Right. You're right." She looked at Amanda. "I would love for you to stay over, Amanda. I've got the guest room cleared out and I even have business-speed Internet for you."

Edward sighed deeply and smiled. "Fine, then we'll all meet you at the agility trial tomorrow morning and then I'll take over after that. We'll use Jacob and Suzy for crowd scanning at public events and continue this level of protection until the killer is captured. Agreed?"

Everyone nodded in agreement.

Edward smiled with great satisfaction. "Now, we can review our investigation."

Nicole walked out with another tray of drinks. "Hey, guys, why so serious?"

"Just enjoying the evening," said Amanda with appalling faked innocence.

After Nicole dropped off the drinks and left the table, Savannah reached into her backpack and pulled out a small tan notebook and a pencil. "I wrote out a copy of our whiteboard."

She flipped a few pages and looked at the sheet. "First, Jacob. Anything else in the applications?"

"Not yet, Miss Savannah. I'm almost done with my analysis. I will come back after Rooney's competition tomorrow morning to finish."

"Is your mom still good with that?"

"Yes."

"That's good," Savannah said, "but I would expect you'll run out of ways to shuffle the applications, soon."

"Sorry, Keith, I forgot to ask about your knee."

"I've got it slathered in Ben-Gay, but I'm still gimpy," said Keith.

Savannah looked at her notes and shook her head from side to side. "You know what?" She closed the little notebook. "I'm really sick of this. We're down to either Wanda or Vincent for Megan's murder—maybe it's even Leon. But honestly, for tomorrow, I don't even want to think about it. I need a break and Rooney needs to have his day."

Her posse smiled in agreement.

Chapter 26

Saturday Morning

It was a beautiful, refreshingly cool morning at Vinoy Park. Perfect for the agility meet—not too hot, not too cool. It was Goldilocks perfect.

Amanda and Savannah parked near the public pool a little north of the park and lugged their mountain of stuff down to the registration table, where a keen teenager checked them off his list and handed back a bag of materials. Most of the participants had already arrived and staked out the best spots to chill while other events were held.

They walked over to the outer edge of the encampment and settled themselves and Rooney for an anxious morning waiting for the puppy trials to begin.

"This is nice." Amanda looked around the park from the comfort of her folding chair. She saw a stuffed picnic basket, and an ice chest tightly filled with water for dogs, water and beverages for humans, along with snacks for dogs and snacks for humans. "What's next?"

Sitting down for the first time since the alarm went off at 5:00 A.M. for a short run to calm Rooney before the competition, Savannah answered, "I'm not exactly sure. This is my first meet. I think the organizers announce when the owners can walk the course. I'll need you to keep Rooney here."

"Why?"

"The dogs aren't allowed in the ring before they run the course."

"Makes sense."

"Yep, that makes it fair for—"

A loudspeaker blared, "Owners of the small puppy category, report to the judges' table."

"That's the group in front of us. Rooney is in the large puppy class." Rooney lifted his ice blue eyes her way. She bent down and snuggled his head. "You don't act like a puppy, do you?"

"Puppy talk is weird." Amanda opened the ice chest. "How long until your turn?"

"I think it's ten minutes for each class."

Savannah relaxed in the folding chair and looked around at the crowd. She recognized one of the couples that were members of her training class. She waved a hello and they returned in kind. The entire area resonated with a tailgate party ambiance and the kind of excitement she imagined came before a stag or fox hunt in times past.

Before she knew it, her group was called to the judges' table. They checked her credentials and she signed in. The registrant pointed to the ring and Savannah walked toward the enclosure.

Rats, I've been an idiot. What was I thinking? Instead of lollygagging, I should have watched the other owners. What should I do?

She entered the ring and moved away from the entrance and waited quietly until several more owners arrived. She watched as they stood in the center of the course sizing up the obstacles. Then some of them began running the course as if they were coaching their dog.

Getting the gist of it, Savannah ran the course several times so that under the pressure of competition she wouldn't make a wrong turn. She was about to run it again when a whistle signaled the end of the walk-around.

When she returned to their little nest, Rooney wiggled a warm welcome.

"How was it?" Amanda handed her a steaming cup of coffee poured from an ancient thermos bottle.

"I'm so feeling like a rube. You know, I might have taken a little time to figure out what these meets were like. I'm not sure Rooney will have a chance."

"Sure, sure," smirked Amanda. "You've had loads of time lately. Plenty of time between running a business, creating new classes, handling your dad's final affairs, training a gorgeous puppy, and running down clues for a murder case. Yep, plenty of time."

"I hate it when you're right." Savannah looked across the park and sighed deeply. A motley pair was making its way onto the grass and looking bewildered. "There are the guys. Lost, as usual."

Edward and Jacob were obviously scanning the crowd for them. Jacob pointed directly to them after spotting them. He picked up Suzy and started toward their encampment.

Rooney was delighted to see Suzy and they said hello like the buddies they were. Savannah looked up. "Where's Edward? I saw him with you a second ago."

Jacob made a short scan of the area, then pointed. "He wanted to scan the perimeter. There he is."

"He doesn't need to do that." Savannah reached into her backpack and pulled out a red bandana. Waving it wildly, she got Edward's attention. He waved to Savannah and began picking his way through the waiting contestants.

After the guys set up their chairs and everyone finally settled, Savannah moved her chair over slightly toward Edward.

Savannah spoke quite softly. "Thanks for coming. I appreciate the support. Rooney and I will be in the second trial. First up will be the small puppies; then we follow them."

"Where's Keith?"

"I don't know. I think he gave me the wrong hotel. I knocked on the room number and disturbed a young couple. They were quite irritated."

Savannah frowned. "I hope he shows up soon."

Edward stood. "I think I'll take a stroll and see if I can spot anyone suspicious. How long do you think this round will last?"

"No clue. I need to stay for the awards ceremony. It shouldn't be too long. Probably a couple of hours?"

"Is he acting weird or what?" Amanda huffed. "He's coming off all possessive like a jealous lover."

"Amanda! That's not true at all—that's ridiculous."

"He's a healthy male animal and a prime, mating-ready female is within sniffing distance. You are blind if you can't see it. I can see it. What does that tell you?"

Savannah wobbled her head. "I'm not ready for any of this. You know that."

The sound system screeched and the organizers announced the start of the large puppy category.

Savannah, Amanda, and Rooney, who was remarkably calm, walked to the judges' table. Savannah and Rooney presented themselves and checked in. The judge pointed toward the course. "You'll be the third contestant. Stand by the entrance."

Before they reached the holding area, Amanda took Savannah by the arm then stood on her tippy-toes and looked in each nautical direction in turn. "What are you doing?" Savannah asked, then turned to Rooney, who began to growl in a low grumble.

"Rooney? What's wrong, buddy?" As she bent down to pet Rooney, she said, "Amanda, what in heaven's name are you doing?"

"I'm searching for your attacker. That's what we're all here for, remember? Although even if your life wasn't threatened, we would all be here for Rooney. This is awesome."

Rooney growled low again and then looked up at Savannah and whined with a questioning look. "What's wrong, Rooney?" She knelt on one knee and took his face in her hands. "You know how to do this. You're very well trained. Be calm, Rooney, be calm."

Finally, the announcer said, "Savannah Webb with Rooney King, please report to the starting mark."

Savannah led Rooney into the ring and he hopped onto the pause platform with no hesitation. She commanded him to stay with a hand signal and moved to the first obstacle, the hurdle, anticipating the starting whistle. Under her breath she repeated, "Stay, Rooney."

The whistle blew and Rooney exploded over the hurdle and turned right to jump through the tire hoop. Savannah ran beside him as he deftly zoomed over the catwalk. She signaled him around the marker and they headed toward the brush jump, which he cleared with huge air and hopped onto the platform.

"Stay, Rooney." This was a five-second pause, which was particularly challenging for puppies.

Wow! This is amazing. I love it.

Rooney was virtually wiggling from head to tail awaiting her command.

When she finally commanded, "Go," Rooney tore through the weaving flags like a firefighter and scrambled over the seesaw with only a little balance bobble at the center. The next obstacle was the window jump and he whisked through the opening clean and clear.

He is amazing. If I can just get him through the tunnel, we could win this.

She stationed herself at the tunnel entrance and prepared herself to signal him through the opening.

As soon as Rooney hit the ground after the window jump, everything changed.

He stopped dead in his tracks and stiffened on all fours. He put his head in the air and howled like an angry wolf.

Savannah ran back to him from the tunnel entrance. "Come on, Rooney. You can do this." She ran a few feet toward the tunnel. Rooney did not follow.

"Rooney, don't do this. Remember your training." His head was pointed to the crowd and he barked twice in a voice Savannah had never heard. "Rooney! Calm, Rooney!" She could hear the shrill panic in her voice.

Rooney looked at her with pleading eyes, barked again, then jumped over the barrier to the course in one smooth, spectacular leap and dove into the crowd, baying like a hunter.

Savannah screamed, "Rooney!" then tore through the entrance to the course and ran around the outside to the spot where he had jumped. The disruption of the crowd showed her where he had gone and she quickly followed.

Halfway down the park she could see that he was chasing a man dressed in black. The man shoved over a young man and hopped onto his plain black motorcycle, then revved the engine high. Rooney slid to a halt and crouched low. The rider pulled out into traffic and sped down Beach Drive.

What is he doing? Who is that?

Just as she caught up to a wildly barking Rooney and clipped the leash onto his harness, another roar came from behind. It was Edward on his vintage Indian motorcycle giving chase. As he sped by, he hollered, "Call Detective Parker! I think Rooney has picked out the person who attacked you!"

"Who is it?!" she yelled.

"I can't tell!" he yelled back and then began to expertly weave through the heavy traffic. He was only a short block behind the black bike.

Savannah pulled her cell from her back pocket and dialed Detective Parker's direct office number. Luckily, he answered immediately. "Detective Parker, we've got my attacker on the run, and I think he's Megan's killer. Rooney sniffed him out. We don't know who yet, but he's speeding out of town on a black motorcycle. Edward should have him cornered in a few minutes. He's sure to overtake him quickly."

She listened to a string of muffled swearing.

"Rooney picked him out of the crowd. He had the scent when I was attacked. He's the one true witness."

"Stay where you are, Savannah. I'll have a cruiser over there immediately."

"He'll get away. I'll call when we have him."

"Listen to—"

Savannah stowed her phone, then started running at top speed with Rooney toward her car. Amanda and Jacob came running up from the other side of the park. Savannah shouted, "I saw Edward take off. We need to help."

They piled into the Mini and drove after them. She didn't think it would take very much distance for Edward to overtake the killer.

Be careful, be careful. Please be careful.

As she drove up the brick street on the waterfront, she saw the Indian motorcycle parked by the curb and the black motorcycle was lying on its side less than a quarter mile up Beach Drive. It was almost exactly where Savannah had been attacked. She could see Edward chasing the hooded man on foot. She parked behind them and let Rooney out of the car. "Get him, boy. Get that bad man."

Rooney took off like a gray rocket and in seconds overtook Edward to grab the hooded man by the seat of his pants. Tugging mightily, Rooney pulled the man to the ground and sat on him. Edward stood with his head down, hands on his knees, panting like a steam engine. A police siren sounded in the background and was getting closer. Savannah caught up to them as Edward grabbed the man's hood and pulled it away from his face.

"Keith?" Savannah's voice was shaking. "You killed Megan? Why?"

Chapter 27

Saturday Noon

"So this is what pandemonium means," Savannah whispered under her breath, which really wasn't necessary for all the yelling. Detective Parker had ordered the posse downtown to the police department and they were stuffed into a conference room waiting for him to return.

The yelling started as soon as they entered. Amanda was yelling at Edward for not putting on his helmet. Jacob's eyes were wide and Suzy's eyes were wider. Rooney wasn't helping by barking at everyone.

"Hush, guys." Savannah rapped the table with her knuckles. "Calm down. This isn't helping and you're alarming the dogs." She waved a hand to the chairs surrounding the long wooden table. "Sit."

Rooney immediately sat to attention. Everyone

laughed and began settling into the comfortable office-style chairs.

Amanda and Jacob sat across from Edward and Savannah. Jacob looked down at Suzy, who had nestled under his chair. She looked up at him calmly.

Savannah turned to Edward. "This pretty much closes the case."

"It does provide closure for Megan's family." He looked into Savannah's eyes. "I'm sure they're in extreme shock."

"Do you think it would be appropriate if I dropped by to offer my sympathy? I didn't feel like I could do that while I was a suspect."

Edward nodded. "I think that would be very much appreciated. They need to know why she was chosen to receive the Best of Show award."

Savannah nodded. "Not only that, I think I can tell them that she finally found her true inspiration within her own heart. I think that's why her last piece is so vibrant—she had found herself."

"You sure you don't want to go to Seattle and teach there?"

"I admit that I had a few homesick moments. I miss the hot glass. I miss the team environment and I miss—"

"The beer or the coffee?" Edward leaned into the table to look around.

Savannah laughed. "Nope, we have those here."

The door opened and Detective Parker stepped

into the conference room followed by Officer Boulli.

"Good afternoon." He sat at the head of the conference table and Officer Boulli wobbled his way down to the foot. Detective Parker placed a fat manila folder on the table and waited until Officer Boulli squeezed into the chair.

"Thanks to you, Keith is writing up his confession to the murder of Megan Loyola and also for the attack on Savannah."

Amanda shot her hand up into the air. "Do you know why he did it?"

Detective Parker nodded slightly. "Let's start with that." He opened the manila folder to a sheet of scribbled notes. "Keith worked with Megan at the Duncan McCloud Gallery during her residency. Apparently, their relationship began after Megan broke it off with Leon."

"But her team members were Leon and Vincent during the hot shop work," Savannah said. "Her past behavior was to create new work with her newest lover. You can't have enemies when you're handling molten glass in tight quarters."

"Apparently that was a big issue. Megan had taken Keith as her lover right before she perfected the process that produced the red torso. Typical of her past behavior, she dropped him after the masterpiece was ready for entry into the Spinnaker Art Festival. That was the breaking point."

Amanda spoke up, "That's cruel. She used her lovers for inspiration during the heat of creation and then tossed them aside after the passion no longer fed her work. Cruel and sad."

"So, a sexual relationship had that much influence on her work?" Edward's eyes widened with disbelief.

Savannah nodded. "Yes, especially when the work is cutting edge. Everything in your life influences it. She had found a way to harness that initial passion. That's why her works were so powerful."

Detective Parker cleared his throat. "Unfortunate for the lovers. This time she picked one too mature to submit meekly to her cruelty. Keith was infuriated by Megan's rejection and they argued that Saturday night."

"Why didn't anyone hear them?" Jacob asked.

"Good question." Detective Parker looked over at a calm Jacob, who held Suzy up so she could see everyone. "The argument was behind Megan's exhibit tent after the other exhibitors had buttoned up their tents. Anyway, when he realized that she wasn't going to take him back, he says he became overcome by a red fury and shoved her into a nearby vase and when she fell the shard caused the fatal injury. I don't believe he came to the booth planning to kill her."

"So, it was a crime of passion," Savannah said.

"It could also have been a crime of opportunity. In any case, he should have called for help at the time it occurred. Instead, he went to great lengths to cover up the accident."

"If it was only about their relationship, why keep it quiet?" Edward spoke so softly everyone leaned forward. "Was it also about the new process for curing the copper ruby glass?"

"That was a big part of it. He said Megan wouldn't agree to be his co-inventor in the patent application for the improved process. Combined with the relationship rejection, it pushed him to violence."

Savannah couldn't keep still. "What about Wanda? We know about the missing money. Will she be arrested?"

Detective Parker looked down and then directly at Officer Boulli, at the other end of the table. "That investigation is ongoing so I can't discuss it with you. I can, however, tell you that our office is taking the matter very seriously. We are taking steps to ensure that an audit of the Spinnaker Art Festival books will expose any irregularities you"—he smiled at Jacob—"might have discovered."

Detective Parker slowly closed the manila folder and placed his folded hands on its front cover. "I thank you for your assistance. We were close to arresting Keith and I'm certain we would have done so within a few more hours, but you managed to beat us to the punch by luring him to the agility meet."

He smiled at each of them with a cold glint in his eyes. "Now, for the lecture."

Chapter 28

Sunday Noon

Savannah's small deck covered by a wooden pergola was barely large enough for the celebration party. Amanda had taken possession of the swinging hammock chair while Jacob stood at the far end watching Rooney and Suzy play among the agility obstacles.

As part of the celebration, Savannah had rashly offered a cookout and stood flipping burgers and hot dogs at the charcoal grill that had been her father's entertainment station. She smiled as she remembered how he would tell funny stories about clients and students and have everyone in stitches. Good times.

"When's Edward getting here?" Jacob asked.

"He should be here already." Savannah started toasting the hamburger and hot dog buns. "He said he might be late." Her cell phone rang. She looked at the caller ID and answered. "Hello, this is Savannah Webb. Yes, I certainly enjoyed being a judge. That's very kind. Thanks for letting me know. Bye."

Amanda stood next to Savannah and began preparing platters to receive the food. "Was that someone from the Spinnaker committee?"

"Yes." She started transferring the hamburgers and hot dogs to a waiting platter. "It seems that Wanda's replacement on the committee was impressed with not only my judging skills, but our sleuthing skills as well. He's confident that the committee will appoint me as next year's glass art judge."

Amanda handed her the wicker basket for the buns, but froze. "Next year's judge?" She put the basket on the side shelf attached to the grill and started unloading the buns from the grill. "That's great, I think. Hopefully, it will be an ordinary event."

"That's not all." They carried the meat and buns over to the food table. "He has also appointed Webb's Glass Shop as the referral studio for teaching beginning glass students."

"Really?"

"Yes, it's a major coup over Frank Lattimer's shop. He's had that referral for many years, since he's so close to the committee downtown."

"Your dad would be so proud."

Savannah smiled and felt warm from her chest to her ears. "Yes. Yes, he would be proud."

They placed the food on the table and Amanda scrunched her brow. "Who is stepping in to take over Wanda's responsibilities?"

"It's one of the selection committee members

that you met at the St. Petersburg Yacht Club meeting."

"I met several." She smiled and shook her head. "You're stringing this out. This is giving you a real tickle, isn't it?"

"Yes, it is. His name is Wilson Barnes."

"I remember him. He seemed very kind and sensible—neither was a quality that was prized this past year. That is going to be great for next year's Spinnaker Art Festival. I'm so pleased."

Hands on her hips, Savannah surveyed the food table and adjusted the placement of the paper plates and condiments. She heard the front-door bell. "Okay, guys, go ahead. That will probably be Edward."

Savannah opened the door to find Edward standing in front of a smiling older man and plump maternal woman. Edward held a red enamelware dish and wore a sheepish grin.

"Savannah, I've taken the bold liberty of inviting my parents to your cookout. As an apology, I've brought a pot of Mum's famous chili."

She laughed like a tickled baby, then said, "You mean your pub's 'World Famous Royal Chili' "—she finger quoted—"is a family recipe? Priceless."

Barging around her son, the woman said, "Hello, pet, I'm Glenda Morris and this is my husband as well as Edward's dad, Ron. We're so delighted to finally meet Edward's sweetheart."

Savannah's hand flew to her throat and she shot an alarmed look at Edward. "Oh." She quickly took Glenda's hand. The next shock was

her soft, almost feathery handshake. Then Ron
reached out a weathered hand and she received
a hearty handshake along with an enthusiastic
kiss on the cheek.

Edward grimaced and hustled them out to
the deck, where he immediately proceeded to
introduce them to everyone individually. They
seemed delighted to be meeting Edward's friends.

*What has he been saying to his parents? What have
I been saying to him?*

After the bustle of doling out the burgers,
dogs, and chili, Savannah, puzzled by Edward's
furious signaling, joined him at the far end of
the small backyard.

He whispered loudly, "Savannah, I don't know
what to say. I don't know where my mum gets
these ideas. Are you angry?"

She took a deep breath, then said, "No, I'm
not angry; I was surprised."

"So, the idea is not precisely repugnant?"

"Well, let's just say that I'm not opposed."
Then, to show him exactly what she meant, she
kissed him deep and true.

FUSED GLASS GLOSSARY OF TERMS

Fused glass is glass that has been fired (heat-processed) in a kiln at a range of high temperatures from 593°C (1,099°F) to 816°C (1,501°F). There are three main distinctions for temperature application and the resulting effect on the glass.

Firing in the lower ranges of these temperatures (593°C–677°C or 1,099°F–1,251°F) is called *slumping*. Firing in the middle ranges of these temperatures (677°C–732°C or 1,251°F–1, 350°F) is considered *tack fusing*. Firing the glass at the higher spectrum of this range (732°C–8 16°C or 1,350°F–1,501°F) is referred to as a *full fuse*.

All of these techniques can be applied to one glasswork in separate firings to add depth, relief, and shape.

Coldworking is a collective term for the many techniques used to alter or decorate glass after the annealing, or cooling, process is complete. This includes grinding, polishing, cutting, engraving, etching, sandblasting, stippling, and more.

Glass casting is the process in which glass objects are cast by directing molten glass into a mold, where it solidifies. The technique has been used since the Egyptian period. Modern cast glass is formed by a variety of processes such as kiln casting or casting into sand, graphite, or metal molds.

INFORMATION ABOUT FUSED GLASS INSTRUCTION

Making gifts of glass is my favorite hobby. My husband and I have a large kiln that we use to fuse glass and make cheese trays out of wine bottles. Most stained-glass shops offer workshops on how to make plates, platters, jewelry, and my favorite: Christmas ornaments. Webb's Glass Shop is inspired by the real-life Grand Central Stained Glass business owned by our good friends Bradley and Eloyne Ericson. Their website is: http://www.grandcentralstainedglass.com.

Find a class in your area by searching the web for fused glass classes in your city.

My husband and I have a glass studio in a cottage behind our house. We're usually making gifts for friends and family. Our latest project is etching my Webb's Glass Shop Mystery cover art onto crystal books. They are gorgeous and I usually have one with me when I have an event. To see the steps we take in making one, go to https://www.hobbyreads.com.

ABOUT
THE JEWELRY

Like Savannah, I make fused glass jewelry to complement my outfits and to use up the leftover odds and ends of the various glass projects that my husband and I create. I post new pieces to my Cheryl Hollon Writer Facebook page. Sometimes, I offer them as a giveaway to thank friends for sharing news about the Webb's Glass Shop Mystery series. Stop by and see what's cooking in the kiln.

Don't miss the next book
in the Webb's Glass Shop Mystery series,

Cracked to Death

Available wherever books and ebooks
are sold in July 2016!

**When a treasure hunt leads to deadly plunder,
it's up to glass shop owner Savannah Webb
and her trusty investigative posse
to map out the true motives of a killer . . .**

It's the dog days of summer in St. Petersburg,
Florida, and Webb's Glass Shop proprietor
Savannah Webb has an eco-friendly plan to
help locals escape the heat—a recyclable
bottle-crafting workshop taught by reticent
store manager Amanda Blake. Turns out,
the class is a bigger smash than expected,
thanks in part to a pair of staggeringly old
bottles brought in by snorkeler Martin Lane . . .

Linked to a storied pirate shipwreck, the relics
definitely pique Savannah's interest.
But intrigue turns to shock when Martin's
lifeless body washes ashore the next morning,
another glass artifact tucked in his dive bag.
With cell phone records connecting Amanda
to the drowning, Savannah must voyage
through unchartered territory to exonerate
her colleague and capture the twisted
criminal behind Martin's death . . .